Woof, There It Is

Deborah Gregory

JUMP AT THE SUN
HYPERION PAPERBACKS FOR CHILDREN
NEW YORK

Fashion credits: Photography by Charlie Pizzarello. Models: Mia Lee, Sabrina Millen, Sonya Millen, Imani Parks, and Brandi Stewart. On Imani (Dorinda): blue top by XOXO. On Brandi (Chanel): vest by Trash & Vaudeville. Dresses by Betsey Johnson. Skirts by P. Fields and Rebecca Taylor. Dog collars by Le Chien. Hair accessories by HEAD DRESS. Hair by Julie McIntosh. Makeup by Lanier Long and Deborah Wallace. Fashion styling by Nole Marin.

Printed in the United States of America

First Edition

5 7 9 10 8 6 4

This book is set in 12-point Palatino.

ISBN: 0-7868-1424-1

Library of Congress Catalog Card Number: 99-67723.

For my friend Laura,
whom I adora,
And her pooch Pongo,
who plays the bongo!

The Cheetah Girls Credo

To earn my spots and rightful place in the world, I solemnly swear to honor and uphold the Cheetah Girls oath:

- Cheetah Girls don't litter, they glitter. I will help my family, friends, and other Cheetah Girls whenever they need my love, support, or a *really* big hug.

- All Cheetah Girls are created equal, but we are not alike. We come in different sizes, shapes, and colors, and hail from different cultures. I will not judge others by the color of their spots, but by their character.

- A true Cheetah Girl doesn't spend more time doing her hair than her homework. Hair extensions may be career extensions, but talent and skills will pay my bills.
- True Cheetah Girls *can* achieve without a weave—or a wiggle, jiggle, or a giggle. I promise to rely (mostly) on my brains, heart, and courage to reach my cheetah-licious potential!
- A brave Cheetah Girl isn't afraid to admit when she's scared. I promise to get on my knees and summon the growl power of the Cheetah Girls who came before me—including my mom, grandmoms, and the Supremes—and ask them to help me be strong.
- All Cheetah Girls make mistakes. I promise to admit when I'm wrong and will work to make it right. I'll also say I'm sorry, even when I don't want to.
- Grown-ups are not always right, but they are bigger, older, and louder. I will treat my teachers, parents, and people of authority with respect—and expect them to do the same!

- True Cheetah Girls don't run with wolves or hang with hyenas. True Cheetahs pick much better friends. I will not try to get other people's approval by acting like a copycat.
- To become the Cheetah Girl that only *I* can be, I promise not to follow anyone else's dreams but my own. No matter how much I quiver, shake, shiver, and quake!
- Cheetah Girls were born for adventure. I promise to learn a language other than my own and travel around the world to meet my fellow Cheetah Girls.

Chapter 1

Thank gooseness, we have *finally* reached cruising altitude, after kadoodling for almost the whole night on the ground because of a tropical rainstorm named "Furious Flo."

That's right, Kats and Kittys: the Cheetah Girls are flying the friendly skies together, for our first time as crew! Our destination: Hollywood, California, where we're scheduled to give the most cheetah-licious performance of our very young lives, at the world-famous Tinkerbell Lounge on Sunset Boulevard.

There are going to be record-industry types in attendance, and their job is to determine if we've got the flava that they savor. We've *got* to sing our little hearts out, in order to pounce on an "op" that may not knock twice, if you know what I'm saying.

The more I think about going to Cali, the tighter I clutch the plane ticket I've been holding in my grubby little paw. This showcase could be the beginning of a dream come true, or it could turn out to be a "Nightmare on Sunset Boulevard"!

Speaking of clutching my ticket—next thing I know, I'm clutching for my lunch tray, which is bouncing up and down along with the rest of the plane!

"Is everything okay, ladies?" the flight attendant asks me and my mom. Mom's in the seat next to me, looking over the bills and receipts for her business, Toto in New York . . . Fun in Diva Sizes. Now she looks the flight attendant up and down.

I look at her, too. The attendant is wearing a big black velvet bow on top of her ponytail. She's really pretty.

"Yes, everything is okay," I say with a big smile. "I like your bow!"

"Thank you," the attendant says, like she really means it. Her pretty green eyes are sparkling as she gives me a little wave and heads on down the aisle.

Mom puts down the bills she's been looking at and says in an exasperated tone, "Galleria, honey, would you *please* put the plane ticket away so you don't lose it?"

I stare one last time at my name—Galleria Garibaldi—on the well-pawed plane ticket before I slide it into the flap pocket of my cheetah carry-on bag. Then I shove the bag under the seat. *I still can't believe the Cheetah Girls are going to Hollywoood!*

Of course, it was Mom who hooked it up. Well, not the *whole* thing, but here's the Hollywood wheel-a-deala:

Mom gets her wigs styled by Pepto B., who also does Kahlua Alexander's hair. (Yes, *that* Kahlua.) While Kahlua was getting her hair done for her latest movie project, *Platinum Pussycats*, we, the Cheetah Girls, showed up at Pepto B.'s salon, and rocked it to the doggy bone! "The Platinum Pussycat" was so taken with our cheetah-licious ways that *she* in turn arranged for the Cheetah Girls to perform in a "New Talent Showcase" sponsored by her record label, Def Duck Records.

But, believe me, we've already paid the pied

piper in full. On the night we're supposed to fly, Furious Flo blows into the Big Apple, causing most airline flights to be canceled. Not only did we have to spend six hours in John F. Kennedy Airport, but we also had to sit in the plane, on the runway, for two more hours before takeoff! By the time we took off, we were so kaflempt, we were ready to jump out of the plane window, rent a hot-air balloon, and head to Oz instead!

But like I said before, at last we're finally out of the Twilight Zone now, and safely on our way. They just served us some "lunch," even though it's about sunrise. I guess they got all messed up in their meal schedule when the plane got delayed.

I'm now happily lost in unwrapping my meal, 'cuz I'm supa-dupa hungry-poo. My mom isn't even touching her food. She's just staring at her receipts, shaking her head and frowning.

I can see she's worried. I know things have gotten kaflooeyed at the boutique—ever since Mom started working full-time as the Cheetah Girls' manager. She *had* to hire someone else to manage the store for her, but she almost ended up hitting him with her cheetah purse! The business is Mom's brainchild, even though my dad runs the factory and gives his heart and soul. *But Mom has to control everything.*

I sure hope we get a record deal out of performing in the showcase. If the Cheetah Girls can finally start bringing in some duckets, that would take the pressure off my mom and dad. All I've done lately is take duckets out of the bucket.

Suddenly, there's a pinging sound, and the pilot's voice comes on over the speakers. "Ladies and gentlemen, we're going to be experiencing some turbulence. Please buckle your seat belts and remain seated until further notice."

Uh-oh. Turbulence. I know what that means. It means we still haven't outrun Furious Flo! I buckle myself in, but while I'm doing it, the plane starts bucking like a wild horse. Before I can grab it, my "lunch" is in my *lap*!

"Yaaaa!!!!" I scream. There goes my new cheetah blouse!

The flight attendant rushes over to help. I don't know how she can walk so easy like that, with the plane doing push-ups and swinging left and right.

"Here," she says, offering me a wet towel. Then she gets down and starts scooping up all the food that spilled. Luckily, most of it is still in the plastic container. Unluckily, the part that isn't has spoiled the booti-ful cheetah blouse my mom made me. I *know* this brown gravy stain is not coming out, and I can see the worry lines in my mom's forehead getting deeper every second.

Leaning forward in my seat, I do a quickie check on my crew, to see how they're weathering the storm. It doesn't seem to be bothering Chuchie one bit. She is bopping her head, listening to her Walkman, like nothing is happening. That's Chanel Simmons for you. She's done a lot of flying with her mom to different places, so I guess she's used to this kind of thing.

I am, too—*usually*. I pull a blanket over my blouse, so Chanel won't see my gravy train.

At least I never get *sick* on airplanes. I guess you could say I was born to travel. See, Mom traveled all over the world when she was a runway model. And every summer, ever since I can remember, she and Dad and I have been going to Italy, to see my "Nona in Bologna."

Nona means grandmother in Italian. See, my dad grew up in Bologna, which is in the northern part of Italy, in a region called Emilia-Romagna, stretching east to west across the top of Italy's boot. Lucky for me, he came to America and met my mom. The rest, as they say, is history—or *my*story, to be exact. *My* story.

Next to Chuchie, Dorinda Rogers, or Do' Re Mi as we call her, has her nose in a book—just like she's at home, and at the library—one of her favorite hanging spots. The plane is doing the Macarena or something, and Dorinda, who has never flown in her life, is acting like she's just chillin'!

I don't know why, but suddenly I'm starting to feel a little funny inside. It's crazy—like I said, I never get sick on planes. Maybe it's all the pressure of the showcase we've got coming up, or maybe it's feeling like if we turn stinkeroon, I'll be letting my mom down. Whatever—between that and Furious Flo whipping the plane around, I'm kinda glad I didn't get to eat my lunch. I lean back, taking a deep sigh, and let the air that has been churning in my stomach "fly away."

I take out a wad of bubble gum, and start doin' the chomp-a-roni on it—which I know Mom doesn't appreciate, but right now, it's either chomp or stomp.

Speaking of which, just as my stomach starts to calm down, *another* natural disaster strikes: Aquanette and Anginette Walker, those fabulous Walker twins from Houston, who make up a *très* important two-fifths of the Cheetah Girls equation, start barfing up their BBQ, like bowwows gone bonkers!

Leaning over the back of my seat to witness the twins' latest performance, I can't help but get on their case like mace—even though a few seconds ago, I wasn't feeling much better than they are. "That's what you get for pretending you weren't scared," I heckle them. "Now you're paying the Boogie Man in full!"

Chanel isn't having the twins' theatrics either. "*Cuatro yuks!* Jeez, pleez, give a *señorita* some notice next time, before you serve us your *lonchando*," she moans. Then she covers her face with the cheetah throw Mom lent her, to fight the big chill left by Furious Flo.

"You didn't have to eat the pig a*nd* the poke—and that's no joke!" Do' Re Mi groans.

The three of us always gang up on the twins. Three against two—what can they do, right? Of course, it's all in snap heaven, and the twins don't seem to mind. They just think we're funny—most of the time, they laugh louder than we do! And after all, I guess it isn't the twins' fault they have such weak stomachs. Angie says they get sick whenever they ride elevators above the tenth floor. And it's even worse when, like today, they've just eaten when it happens!

Cheez whiz, what a crew I've got: Do' Re Mi has never been on an airplane before, and the twins have never been out of the country. Never mind though: as soon as the Cheetah Girls get off the ground in more ways than one, we are gonna travel all over the world together, and sing to peeps on two legs and four.

Now I feel bad for embarrassing Aqua and Angie. I reach over the back of my seat and stroke Aqua's bob back into place. It's sticking up like a pinwheel because of all the static in the plane cabin, and I know the twins are very fussy about their hair looking "coiffed."

"You'd better put on that stocking cap before we land," I giggle. "Your hair looks like it's going through electric shock treatment."

Aqua doesn't say anything back, of course, because she's still putting the barf pedal to the metal, and breathing heavy into the paper bag supplied by the airline.

"Didn't you two take your Cloud Nine tablets?" Do' Re Mi asks the twins, like she's a flight attendant or something. So that's why she isn't feelin' it like I am! I'll bet Chuchie took them, too!

Angie looks up, holding the barf bag around her mouth, and shakes her head. "No, we didn't!" Her big brown eyes look puffy, like Popeye's. Aqua finally raises her head up out of the bag, and coughs right at us.

"Uuugh, check it, don't fleck it, Aqua," I moan, covering my mouth in case some alien barf specks float in my direction.

Mom looks up from doing her accounting, and hisses in an annoyed voice, *"Basta!"*

I'll show *her* "enough"—'cuz I haven't even *started* yet on Aqua and Angie. I look at Mom and start sulking. I *hate* when she embarrasses me in front of my crew! Not that Aqua or Angie understood what Mom said, but it wrecks my flow, you know what I'm saying?

Usually, Mom sleeps like a bear, and you couldn't wake her if there was a flood nipping at her heels. Then I realize—she isn't wearing those funny-looking earplugs she usually wears when we fly. That's why she can hear everything.

I grimace at Mom, who's gone back to her work. Then I look down at my hands, and notice that my nails are already chipped!

Leaning down for my carry-on bag, I take out my bottle of S.N.A.P.S. nail polish, and flip the tray down again from the back of the seat in front of me. Steadying the bottle of nail polish like an acrobat, I wield the polish brush across the surface of my nails to cover the chips.

"Miss, you can't polish your nails on the airplane. You'll have to put that away," says the flight attendant, coming up to me. "It's against the rules. Some passengers are allergic to the fumes."

Hmph! Little Miss "Bow" Peep, wrecking my flow. Now I don't like her hairdo anymore! Cheez whiz, a little bit of "*pow!*" nail polish is gonna make the plane go "kapow"?

Now Chanel peeps her head over at me,

smirking. Then she sees the big gravy stain on my blouse, and she gives me a look, like "*Ay, Dios, mamacita*, what did you do?!"

I look away from her, furious. Ooooo, that little Miss Cuchifrito! Wait till we land—I'm gonna get her back good in Hollywood!

Chapter 2

The flight to Los Angeles from New York is five hours long, but it seems like I've been snoozing forever. I see now that the flight attendants are coming around with "breakfast." Good. I'm real hungry by now, since I never did eat my "lunch." I wonder if the Walker twins will feel like eating while we're still airborne. . . .

I look at my Miss Wiggy watch. New York and Cali are in two different time zones. That is such a cool thing. Tomorrow night, L.A. time, the Cheetah Girls will be off to see the Wizard—the wonderful Wizard of Hits—at the Tinkerbell Lounge!

It's eleven o'clock in the morning in New York. That means Dad is probably drinking his fourth cup of espresso of the morning right now, and bossing everybody at the factory around. Here in Cali, however, it's only eight o'clock in the morning.

"You think they've got a pool in the hotel?" I ask Mom, smoothing one of the hairs on her wig back into place.

"I'm sure you'll find out as soon as we get there," Mom says, then yawns, twirling her cheetah eye shades in her hand. I guess she tried to sleep, but it doesn't look like she succeeded. She's pretty punchy, and I guess it's partly my fault for dragging her into this.

Not that I even asked her to be our manager. She volunteered. But if she hadn't done it, the Cheetah Girls would have been history. So it's like she did it for me. And all it's brought her so far is headaches and baggy eyes. Not one ducket in the bucket. Well, the showcase at the Cheetah-Rama doesn't really count.

"Ooh, look, the clouds are so white they look like cotton candy!" Chanel coos. "*Gracias* gooseness, Flo isn't here!"

"Girls, don't forget to set your clocks three

hours back," Mom says, perking up. "We don't want to be three hours early for *anything*."

Believe me, no matter how worried she is about her coins, Mom is excited about taking us all to L.A. She has every hour of our trip scheduled, like she's a librarian and we're books on loan—we'll be fined if we're not back on time!

Thank gooseness, the "New Talent Showcase" is not until tomorrow night. That gives us one whole day and a half of fun in the sun—or at least in the indoor pool at the hotel—and the chance to check out Hollywood—the 'Wood.

Of course, we do have to spend some time doing our homework, so we can make up for the day of school we'll be missing. Chuchie, Do', and I all go to Fashion Industries High School together. The Walker twins go to LaGuardia Performing Arts High. They've got it like that.

Of course, if Chuchie hadn't chickened out of our audition, we might've had it like that, too. Of course, if we'd gotten into LaGuardia, we wouldn't have met Do' Re Mi, and who knows if the Cheetah Girls would've ever happened.

Still, maybe one day we'll all be going to LaGuardia together. It's one of my dreams. That, and a record deal for the Cheetah Girls, of course!

After we land, we are bustling along in the *très* busy LAX airport, which is even bigger than JFK airport in New York.

"Look, yo, there's a guy with a sign with your last name!" Do' Re Mi exclaims. The man holding the sign is wearing a black suit with a black hat.

"That's the driver," Mom says, waving at him.

"Mrs. Garibaldi?" the man asks, like he isn't sure.

"Hi there, I'm Mrs. Garibaldi," Mom says, relieved. "I'm so glad you waited. Our flight was delayed for six hours because of Furious Flo. What's your name?"

"Pedro. Welcome to Los Angeles," he says with a smile. His mustache is so neat it looks like he drew it on with a pencil. "I've been hearing all about Furious Flo on the radio."

"She almost wrecked our *flow*, that's for sure," Do' Re Mi says with a sigh.

I put my arms around her. "I'm so proud of you—you didn't barf once!" But what I'm thinking is, Next time, share the Cloud Nine tablets!

Pedro waits to get our luggage off the carousel. I notice a big sign that says: *SOME LUGGAGE LOOKS ALIKE. MAKE SURE YOU READ THE TAG CAREFULLY BEFORE YOU GRAB YOURS.*

"Hmmph. *Our* luggage doesn't look like anybody else's," I chuckle to my crew, as I see Mom's cheetah suitcases coming around the bend of the carousel.

All of a sudden, Do' Re Mi's old orange plaid suitcase comes out of the chute. It hits the bottom of the carousel and pops open, dragging her clothes behind it—cheetah bloomers and all!

"No! No! I'm not having it!" Do' Re Mi groans, putting her hand up over her eyes.

Pedro comes to the rescue. "Don't worry, *señorita*, I fix for you!" he says. He starts pushing people out of the way to get Dorinda's suitcase and her floating clothes before they go around the baggage carousel once again, for the whole crowd to see.

Just our luck—at that exact moment, some

bozo wearing a Lakers cap beats Pedro to the punch. As Do' Re Mi's pooped-out suitcase goes by him, he grabs a pair of cheetah undies, and holds them high above his head. Then he yells, "Yo, who these belong to?"

I can hear some other guys laughing, and looking around to see who's gonna claim the cheetah underwear.

"Oh, so now I get it, they've got bozos out here, too," I humph. I cross my arms, just waiting to see what the pinhead in the Lakers cap is gonna do with Do' Re Mi's teeny-weeny undies.

Thank gooseness, Pedro pipes right up. "Please to give to me, sir!"

"Oh, it's like that," Pinhead responds, but you can tell he's a little disappointed that he didn't get to meet the owner of the bloomers.

Do' Re Mi looks like she just wants to do an "abracadabra" and disappear up the luggage chute.

Pedro retrieves the undies from Pinhead and grabs Do' Re Mi's suitcase. He places it on the floor and tries to snap it shut, but the latch is broken.

A nice lady walks over to Pedro and hands

him one of Do' Re Mi's undershirts. "Sir, you forgot this one. It didn't get too wrinkled, dear," she adds, looking sympathetically at Do'.

Pedro thanks the lady a thousand times and keeps trying to close the suitcase. Finally, he looks up sheepishly and says, "No fix, *señorita*. I'm sorry."

"That's okay," Do' Re Mi says, her eyes planted downward, as if she's afraid to look up at all the people watching us.

Pedro carefully places Do' Re Mi's suitcase in the luggage cart, then puts ours on top, and pushes the cart along to the lot where he's parked his car. Mom, Pedro, the twins, and Chuchie are already inside the car, a fabulous Town Car limo, when I hear someone calling us from the other side of the parking lot.

"Yo! Cheetah Girls!" I look up to see who it is, and I nearly lose my lunch right there.

"Stak Jackson!" I gasp, as he and his brother, Chedda, come loping toward us, big pointy-toothed grins on their faces. The two of them are a rap group, Stak Chedda. And they're not too cheesy, either. They actually beat us in the Apollo Theatre Amateur Hour Contest.

Yes, we, the fierce Cheetah Girls, actually lost the Apollo Theatre Amateur Contest to these two bozos, who are carrying duffel bags bigger than they are. And now I feel like I'm seeing a mirage. They're even wearing the same yellow satin baseball jackets and caps they had on at the Apollo. Somebody better yell for "*wardrobe!*"

"What are y'all doin' in L.A.?" I ask, thinking that this can't be a "coinky-dinky," a coincidence.

"We wuz just gonna ask y'all the same thing!" Chedda says.

"Um, we're . . ."

Words fail me, as I realize I can't tell the truth. If these two bozos hear about the Def Duck Records showcase, they'll wind up worming their way into it—and we don't want them movin' in on our groove—you know what I'm saying?

"Um . . . we're here to make a music video," I say, wincing. I know it's a fib-eroni, but it's all I can think of at the moment.

"Music video?" Aqua pipes up, oblivious. "Wha— OWW!" she says, as Do' Re Mi gives her a little kick in the shin.

"Um, what are *y'all* doin' out here?" I ask, changing the subject.

"Us? Um, we're . . ." Chedda starts, but Stak cuts him off.

"We're visiting our uncle Dudley," he says. "He's rich, and we're trying to get him to back our act."

"That's dope," I say. "Well, toodles. We gotta go. See you back in the Big Apple."

"No doubt," Stak says. "Oh, by the way," he adds, turning to Do' Re Mi. "Nice cheetah undies." He and his bozo brother crack up, and slap each other a high five.

Dorinda practically sinks into the pavement. These two must have been in the crowd by the carousel!

"Put a lid on it, bozos!" I blurt out, losing my temper. "We can't all be carrying duffel bags!"

Right away, I'm sorry I said it. I know I was only trying to represent my crew, but now I've gone and made Dorinda feel even worse—calling attention to her broken-down suitcase. I could kick myself!

"Come on, yo," I say, putting my arm around her and helping her into the Town Car. "We're out," I tell Stak and Chedda, and get into the car myself.

As I shut the door behind me, I can feel the sense of doom and gloom that has descended upon my crew. "What?" I say. "Just because we happen to run into them out here doesn't mean it's an evil omen or something. It's just a coinky-dinky!"

Silence. I know they don't believe me. All my crew are superstitious, and you know this cannot be a good sign.

"It's so dope that they provided a car for us, isn't it?" I ask, trying to lighten things up, as we pull out of the lot and onto the freeway of loot in sunny Los Angeles.

"This car is *la dopa*!" Chuchie says, beginning to get in the mood. All it takes is a little luxury, and she always perks right up.

"Dag on, look at all those fancy cars we're passin'," Aqua says. "They got some serious money in this town!"

For now, it seems, they've forgotten our little meeting with Stak Chedda. I decide to do the same. So they were on the same plane with us, and saw Do' Re Mi's underwear doing the float. So what? It doesn't mean they're gonna find out about our showcase and crash it.

I decide not to worry. Good for them if their uncle Dudley's rich, and wants to back them. They need all the help they can get in the wardrobe department. Let them think we're out here doing a music video! Ha! That was a pretty good fib-eroni, if I say so myself. Good thing Do' Re Mi stopped Aqua from opening her trap at the wrong time!

I give Do' Re Mi a big hug and start tickling her. I'm trying to get her mind off the suitcase drama, but the way she's still staring at the floor of the car, I don't think I'm succeeding.

"Anything with its wheels firmly planted on the ground is a welcome sight after that plane ride," Mom says, settling into the soft leather seat in front.

"I can't wait to take a nice bubbly bubble bath," I whisper to Chanel, as we enjoy the supa-spacious ride. "Check it, don't wreck it, 'cuz we are V.I.P., yo!"

Chanel starts yapping away to Pedro in Spanish, then tells us that he is "Chicano," which means he is Mexican-American. She says he grew up in East L.A.

"He says they have a lot of Chicanos here—like millions," Chuchie tells us, sucking on her Dolly lollipop.

"We got a lot of Mexicans in Texas, too—they're called Tejanos, right, Angie?" Aqua asks her sister, then burps. "Excuse me," she giggles.

"Yeah, but this place is definitely bigger," Angie responds. They go on to compare which city—Los Angeles or Houston—has the biggest skyscrapers. Thank gooseness the barfing twins have recovered. I don't want anything else to ruin our trip, now that we've come this far. We've had enough drama and kaflamma already!

"It's actually twice the size of New York," Pedro explains.

"Yeah, and I bet *twice* the fun," I giggle, poking Chanel, who is sitting next to me in the back.

"This is kinda like a limo, right?" she whispers back to me.

"It's a Town Car limo," Mom explains.

"I've never been in car with a bar!" Do' Re Mi exclaims, finally perking up. See, Dorinda lives with her foster mother, Mrs. Bosco, and about a million other foster kids, in this little apartment in the projects. She has never been anywhere but New York—I can tell she is supa-excited to be in Cali.

Woof, There It Is

Now we are driving along the freeway into the city. "Wow, they've got trees and mountains everywhere," I exclaim. It looks a lot like the hills in Italy, as a matter of fact. Only all the buildings here are new, not hundreds of years old like over there.

"The City of Angels is definitely more scenic than the Big Apple," Mom says, nodding her head approvingly.

"What's the City of Angels?'" asks Aqua.

"That's what Los Angeles means in Spanish," Chanel coos.

"Oh, that's real nice," Aqua says, smiling like a dumb sugarplum.

"Oooh, look at the birds!" Chuchie says excitedly, looking at the formation of big black birds flying in the sky. "They must be flying south 'cuz winter is coming."

"They don't have real winter out here," I point out.

Then I notice the twins, who both have spooked looks on their faces.

"Look, Aqua," Angie says. "They're spreading their wings."

"Yeah —and?" Aqua retorts.

"Remember what High Priestess Abala

said?" Angie continues. "'Look for the Raven when she spreads her wings.'"

"Who can forget what *she* says?" Aqua humphs. "I'd like to just plain forget *her.*"

"I know," Angie says. "She gives me the creepy-creeps! I wish Daddy would stop seeing her." Then she repeats High Priestess Abala's mysterious prediction for our future in L.A.: "'Look for the Raven when she spreads her wings.'"

I look up at the black birds. "They look like sparrows or blackbirds to me. They're too small to be ravens," I say. But the twins just give each other a scared look.

Man, I hope the high priestess doesn't put the royal whammy on us. It's bad enough she's got the twins' father in a trance of romance! See, he and Mrs. Walker are divorced, and she lives back in Houston, so I guess it's okay he's got a girlfriend. But what a girlfriend!

A few minutes later, we pull up to the Royal Rooster Hotel, on world-famous Hollywood Boulevard. "The Cheetah Girls are definitely about to spread *their* wings, cock-a-doodle-do-style," I say. "That's what I'm talking about!"

Chapter 3

A man wearing a bright blue top hat, and even brighter blue satin tails, opens the big glass door of the Royal Rooster Hotel for us. "Cock-a-doodle-do! How are you this fine morning, ladies?"

We are tickled by his salutation. "We're the swelliest we can ever be, sir!" Do' Re Mi chimes back at him.

"Glad to hear that, miss, and welcome to the Royal Rooster Hotel, where dreams are hatched by the Hollywood batch!"

That sends Chuchie into a fit of giggles. As soon as we get inside, a bellhop in a bright blue suit with gold embroidery on his jacket loads our luggage onto a gold luggage cart.

When he picks up Do' Re Mi's luggage, she apologetically says, "I'm sorry, this one is busted." Then she quickly drapes her jacket over her suitcase, like she's trying to hide it from plain sight.

Walking to the elevator, Angie and Aqua are looking around in awe. "Look at the ceilings," Aqua says in hushed tones. She pokes Angie to get her to look upward, then points over at the mosaics on the wall depicting roosters laying golden eggs, and farmers running after them like they're the cat's meow.

Whether we snag the record deal or not, I think, the Cheetah Girls *definitely* have something to crow about now, because at least we've stayed at the Royal Rooster Hotel!

"Holy cannoli, that reminds me of the mosaics in Venice," I gasp.

Aqua and Angie look at me like they're impressed, which makes me feel a little embarrassed for bragging. "My father has dragged me to museums all over Italy from the time I was two," I offer, waving my hand in the air like I just don't care. "He loves Venetian glass, too," I say, pointing back to the ceiling.

"Oh," Aqua says, nodding her head like she doesn't know what to say.

"You're so lucky, Bubbles," Do' Re Mi says. "You've traveled to places. I wanna go to Italy, too."

"Yeah—wait till you see it. Don't you worry, though, we're gonna have our own Cheetah Girls gondola take us around everywhere!"

Do' Re Mi shrugs her shoulders at Aqua, like she doesn't understand what a gondola is, so I try to divert their attention. I don't want them feeling bad, just because I've lived *"la dolce vita,"* or "the good life," as they say in Italy.

"Look at the gilded columns!" Aqua gushes as we continue on down the hallway. "All that glitters *is* golden."

"Even the elevators are gilded," Mom says, pointing to the glass-walled, gold-trimmed elevators that are shooting up and down the exposed elevator shafts like golden rockets!

All of a sudden, I see fear creep into Aqua's and Angie's faces as they clutch each other's hands. Oopsy, doopsy! I should've told Mom about their fear of elevators! Wait a minute—what if our room is on a high floor? I wonder.

But I guess there's a reason why Mom is our

manager, because she looks right at the twins and asks, "What's wrong? You look like we've just stepped inside Madison 'Scare' Garden instead of the Royal Rooster Hotel."

"Ms. Dorothea, you know we don't want to be any bother at all," Aqua says, "but we don't want to stay on the tippy-top floor, or something like that—if you don't mind? Angie and I are, kinda, well, afraid of heights."

"Darling, don't worry about a thing! That's why I'm your manager. I'll take care of that."

When the front desk clerk informs Mom that our suite is on the 27th floor, she asks him to switch us into two suites on a lower floor.

"You'll have to give us a second then, ma'am, because we don't have anything available right now," the clerk responds.

Oh, swelly, I think, rolling my eyes. Now we've gotta wait for a room, lest the fabulous Walker twins get another barf attack! Pouting, I walk over to the gold brocade Victorian armchair in the lobby, remove the plump pillow, and plop myself down.

Do' Re Mi wanders over, while the rest of the crew waits by the desk with Mom. "I'm starving like Marvin, yo," she moans, then sits on the carpet.

"Cheez whiz, there are roosters everywhere," I say. "It's enough to make anybody hungry!" I hand the pillow to Do' Re Mi so she doesn't hurt her butt. I notice that the pillow is decorated with an embroidered rooster. "I hope that means we're about to lay a golden egg or something!" I say.

"Yeah. I hope so, too. Aren't you scared though—about tomorrow night?" Do' Re Mi asks me, her voice cracking.

Even though I *am* scared, I don't want to tell Do' Re Mi. I don't want her getting any more ideas about leaving the group. It's only been a few weeks since she almost took a job as backup dancer for Mo' Money Monique's national concert tour. If we don't bag a record deal from this showcase, Do' might figure she made the wrong choice. Then the next time an opportunity comes along . . .

No! She *can't* leave the group—I won't let her!

"You think the other acts got it going on more than we do?" Do' Re Mi asks timidly, swallowing my own fears.

"We're not going out like that, Do',"

I humph. "We'll probably have to deal with some more 'burnt toast' bozos, though!" I snicker.

"Like Stak Chedda?" Do' Re Mi asks me. "Those 'bozos' won the Apollo Contest over *us*."

"Word. I bet you that competition was rigged, yo," I say. Not that Stak Chedda was wack or anything. They were pretty dope, but I still think we were better.

Do' Re Mi scrunches her legs up and wraps her hands around them. "I'm so hungry, I could eat some burnt toast right about now!" she says, giggling.

I giggle, too, and we do the Cheetah Girls handshake.

"Girls! Come on, now. We're in there like swimwear!" Mom yells, motioning for us to hop to it like hares. "Seven is our lucky number, girls, and the only thing I want right now is the biggest bubbly bubble bath this town has to offer."

"Grazie," I say. "Thanks for everything, Mom." I give her a big hug, to tell her how much I appreciate all the sacrifices she's making for us.

"Thanks for getting us a room that's not so high up, Ms. Dorothea," Angie says.

"Of course, darling. We don't want the best two-fifths of our group to irritate their precious vocal cords, now, do we?" Mom snickers. Looking at Aqua and Angie, I can tell they would be turning red for sure right now, if they weren't so brown to begin with.

"I'll bet you the bathtub is big enough to dive into," I giggle.

"Well, don't think you're gonna turn into Flipper before *I* do," Mom says, opening the door to suite 777. "And remember, just because we've got adjoining suites doesn't mean I can't keep all four eyes on you, girlinas."

Opening the middle door that connects to the adjoining suite—778—she instructs Aqua, Angie, and Chuchie to put their stuff in the other room. "Dorinda, Galleria, and I are gonna share this one," she instructs us.

Chanel gives me a look like "What's the deal-io, yo?" but I just wink at her. I think Mom wants to keep a closer eye on Dorinda. She's not worried about her goddaughter Chuchie, who sure won't be getting into any trouble sharing a room with the "goody-two-shoes twins"—our latest nickname for Miz Aquanette and Anginette Walker.

"Ooo, looky cookie, we even got a gift basket!" I say, running over to a big gold basket covered in gold cellophane that's sitting on top of the bureau.

What a swelly room. It's decorated in royal blue, red, and gold, just like the lobby. "Ooo, look at the rooster lamps," I say, pointing to the two matching lamps on the nightstands as I tear into the cellophane.

Mom slaps my hand and says, "Lemme open that!" After she rips open the cellophane and pulls out the card, she reads it out loud for us. "'To the Cheetah Girls. Best of luck tomorrow night. Paul Pett, Talent Showcase Coordinator, Def Duck Records.'"

"That's nice," I respond, rubbing the copper head of the rooster lamp like it's Aladdin's lamp. When I turn on the switch, its tortoiseshell glass body glows with orange light.

"Oh, that is *la dopa*!" Chanel coos, coming into the room.

"Chanel, take some chocolate," Mom says, handing her one of the chocolate eggs wrapped in gold foil from the basket.

"Can I take the guava fruit?" Chuchie asks excitedly. Chuchie loves tropical fruits—and she knows the names of all of them. I guess that's her Dominican heritage. "Can I take the chocolate, too, *Madrina*?" she asks, giggling.

"Of course, Chanel. Now, girlinas, we have to get trussed up like turkeys, because we're going to lunch. Then we'll do a little sight-seeing, okay?" Mom says. Hanging up her cheetah coat in the closet, she adds, "Spacious closets—I'm in a better mood already, darling." She looks at me with a fake grimace. "Oh, go on, Galleria, take your bath first. And *don't* use up all the bubble bath!"

I hightail it to the bathroom. It has a pretty royal blue rug, and towels with red- and gold-embroidered roosters. I love the little bottles of stuff they always have in hotel rooms — except for those "one-star bungalows," as Mom calls the cheapie hotel rooms. Actually, we might be staying in one of those hotels right now, if the record company wasn't paying for our rooms and airfare.

The tub is not as big as I pictured it, but it has pretty copper faucets. I throw the cute rubber rooster in the tub, and watch it float as I pour the little shampoo bottles into the tub along with the bubble bath. I never use hotel shampoos on my hair—they're just for girls with *real* straight hair, not kinks like mine.

"Bring on the suds, bring on the suds! Don't be a dud, 'cuz I need a rub-a-dub-dub!" I hum aloud, as I watch the tub fill up with delicious, bona fide bubbles.

"Lemme see how big your tub is," Chuchie says, crowding into the bathroom behind me.

"The same as the one in your room," I say, exasperated.

"No it isn't, *Mamacita*!" Chuchie says, flicking the bubbles at me, like we used to do when we were little. "Bubbles for bubbles!" she coos. We used to mess up the whole bathroom and make Auntie Juanita mad.

Auntie Juanita and my mom used to be close, back when we were little and they were both models. They barely get along these days, but that's because Auntie Juanita has turned a little "tutti frutti" now that she's getting older. It seems like she spends most of her time worrying about getting wrinkles, or losing weight. Not like Mom. All *she* worries about is getting everything done, and then doing *more* things. She never stops till she drops.

"Chuchie, the rooms are *exactly* the same. There is no shame in your game!" I say to my silly half, as I take off my grimy clothes.

"Excuse me, but I have to go try on everything I own now, *está bien?*" Chuchie says, then walks out of the bathroom.

"Yo! We're just going to lunch, not the Sistarella ball!" I call after her.

"Hey," Chuchie giggles, poking her head back into the bathroom. "You never know who we're gonna meet on the Hollywood Walk of Fame."

"You have no shame, Chuchie," I mutter, sliding down into paradise. "The only thing I love more than bubbles is more bubbles!"

"*Está bien*, Bubblehead!" Chuchie says, making fun of my silly nickname.

Whispering loud enough for Chuchie to hear me, I add, "Just make sure the twins don't wear a corny outfit today."

"*Está bien*, Secret Agent Bubbles!" Chuchie giggles, then finally leaves me in peace.

Do' Re Mi is upset because her clothes are

wrinkled. "Don't worry, darling, I'll just call the valet," Mom explains.

"What's a valet?" Do' Re Mi asks, dumbfounded.

"They take care of hotel guests, and cater to their every whim," Mom explains patiently.

"Well, I don't have any whims," Do' Re Mi chuckles, kinda embarrassed. "But I can iron it myself, if they just give me an ironing board."

"No, they'll do it, darling, don't worry," Mom assures her. "You know, girls, it wouldn't hurt to dress cheetah-certified today, even though you're not performing." With that, she goes into the bathroom.

"Okeydokey," I say. "You hear that, Chuchie? Get cheetah-certified or you're fried!" I yell into the open doorway that joins our suites.

Then I step out onto the balcony to take in the view. The first thing I feel is the breeze. "It's not as hot as I thought it would be in Los Angeles. It's actually kinda chilly willy, isn't it? I guess that means we won't be wearing bikinis, huh?" I snicker to Do' Re Mi.

"Yeah. We'd better wear jackets," Do' Re Mi mutters, still trying to smooth out the wrinkles in her clothes.

"You didn't lose any undies, did you?" I whisper to her.

"Yeah," she whimpers. "I did. The bozo probably stuck one in his pocket. I'll bet he's gonna wear it on his head later!" We giggle loudly.

"Ouch! Why can't they make wax that doesn't take off your skin," Mom yells from the bathroom.

Chuchie comes wiggling into our room, still in her underwear and undershirt. "Chuchie, get dressed!" I yell.

"I just wanna help *Madrina,*" she says. "*Madrina,* you should let Princess Pamela wax your mustache."

"Mustache, Chanel? I'm not a gorilla. It's just a little hair on my upper lip," Mom says loudly from the bathroom. "And besides, the last time I let some beauty wizard wax my upper lip, it looked like I had a localized case of the chicken pox!"

"*Madrina,* I'm telling you, Princess Pamela has the magic touch," Chuchie continues.

"That's for sure, 'cuz Dodo has never seemed happier!" Mom quips, and the two of them giggle at their private joke.

I have to agree. Chanel's dad, Dodo, does seem happier now that he is with Princess Pamela instead of Auntie Juanita. But Juanita seems happier, too, now that she is with Mister Tycoon, this supa-gettin'-paid Arab businessman, who lives in Paris and wears a funny mustache and fancy suits.

"Okay, girlinas, what are we wearing? I suggest the cheetah minis, and flats, 'cuz we're gonna do a lot of walking," Mom says, taking out notes from a pink manila folder.

That's my mom. She has probably scheduled everything, like a drill sergeant in the army. Hup, two, lunch! Hup, two, shopping! Hup, two, rehearsal! Hup, two, go to sleep!

"Okeydokey," Do' Re Mi replies.

"And here are our choices for lunching in the City of Angels. We could go to Porcini, for Italian peasant food," Mom says, rifling through her papers some more. "Or we could try some *gorgeous* Cantonese live seafood at Chop, Chop! Or we could go to Bombay Cafe on Santa Monica Boulevard, for 'Yuppie Indian in West L.A.' It says here they have 'wonderful chutneys, uttapams, and masala dosas,'" Mom repeats, looking up after she has read the review from some magazine.

"What is a 'Yuppie Indian'?" Aqua asks, puzzled.

We giggle, then Mom tries to explain, but even she is stumped. "Well, I guess . . . oh, I don't know—some fabulous curry cuisine, I'm sure!"

Chanel is the first to give Mom the look that says, We're *not* taking any passage to India today, *Mamacita*.

Mom is never stumped by our facial expressions, especially Chuchie's. "Humph! Adventurous as ever, are we, Cheetah Girls?" she says. Then she sighs, because even *she* knows when she has been out-kadoodled by my crew.

"I guess you can take the Cheetah Girls out of the jiggy jungle, but you can't take away their animal instincts for, well, barbecued ribs. *Okay*. Aunt Kizzy's Back Porch it is."

We chuckle up a storm, then Do' Re Mi is the first out the door. "Bring on the BBQ!" she yells, whooping it up.

Aqua licks her juicy lips and seconds that motion. "I know that's right!" she says.

Chapter 4

The first thing you notice about "La La Land," as they call L.A., is that there is a whole lot of space. "Peeps are definitely not living like cockroaches out here, like we do in the Big Apple," I comment to Chuchie as we walk down big, beautiful Hollywood Boulevard.

The second thing you notice about La La Land is that there aren't any *people* walking on the tree-lined sidewalks—not to speak of, anyway. Still, Mom *insists* that we walk to Aunt Kizzy's Back Porch, even though we could've called a taxi.

"Look at the mansions," I exclaim, ogling all the dope estates nestled high up in the looming

Hollywood Hills above us.

"I bet you that's where Kahlua lives!" Aqua says excitedly, pointing to a bright yellow mansion with white pillars at the tippy-top of a hill. "That's real nice, ain't it?"

"Yeah," Angie says, then pokes her mouth out. "I wouldn't want to live there, though—what if they had a fire, and you had to get out in a hurry?"

"An earthquake is more like it," Mom says, shivering her shoulders. Mom has gotten a map of Los Angeles that looks more like an encyclopedia, and she is becoming very roadrunnerish about the whole get-around-town thing.

"They have earthquakes here?" Do' Re Mi asks, scrunching up her nose.

"More of them than garage sales, it seems," Mom replies.

That makes all of us *really* quiet, and I can tell Aqua and Angie are a little spooked. When we get to this biggie-wiggie intersection at Hollywood Boulevard and Vine Street, I can see the twins' teeth chattering, because it seems like it's miles to the other side of the intersection.

"We haven't seen one 'blacktress' yet," Do'

Re Mi says to break the silence. "I bet they're probably getting their nails done. Look at all the cars—*they're* the real stars here."

Even though we're afraid to cross, we finally get the nerve up (okay, Mom drags us), but we soon discover, much to our surprise, that drivers here are a *lot* nicer than in New York. This shiny olive-green car with a sparkling chrome jaguar on its front hood stops right in its tracks to let us cross.

"Can you believe that?" Aqua exclaims in sheer amazement. "He let us live!"

"Don't worry, darling, he's more concerned about us bumping into his prized Jaguar than the other way around," Mom humphs.

"Jaguar," Do' Re Mi says, savoring the name of the car like it was the best slice of corn bread she ever bit into. "It's dope. I can't wait to learn how to drive."

"If you lived out here, you would learn fast. *Everybody* out here drives—even the toddlers," Mom explains, adjusting her cheetah shades to get a better look at what she suddenly sees before her eyes.

In the window of Oh, Snaps! Bookstore, there is a big, framed poster of Josephine Baker.

Collecting memorabilia is the only passion Mom has—other than being "large and in charge," of course.

"It's boot-i-ful," Chanel coos.

In this poster, La Baker is wearing a pink sequined gown, and her arms are stretched upward, like she's on top of the world—and I guess she was. Back then, she was the richest, dopest black woman in the world. "Isn't this one *gorgeous,* darling?" Mom asks me, with a touch of sadness in her voice.

"As *gorge-y* as the fifty other ones you own," I coo back. Mom already owns every other Josephine Baker poster on the planet, including the only one signed by the famous French artiste Cous Cous Chemin, in which Josephine is posing with her pet leopard, LuLu.

The leopard is in this poster, too, sure enough—off to the side, and looking like he just ate the canary. "Ooh, *tan coolio.* His collar is even leopard!" Chuchie says, pointing to the poster.

"How do you know the leopard is a he, Chanel?" challenges Dorinda.

"Guess you'll have to go to the history books and find out," I snicker at Do' Re Mi, who is always reading books of one kind or another. Anything you ever want to know, that nosey-nose will go to the library and find out for you.

I sigh wistfully at the kazillion photos of movie stars in the store window. "One day, *our* photo is gonna be in there," I say to my crew.

"That's a cheetah-certified fact," Mom commands. "Well, let's see if you're ready for the big bargaining league, Galleria."

"I'm ready for Freddy," I quip back. See, the only thing Mom likes better than collecting memorabilia is getting it at a bargain price. It's called "the fine art of snaggled-tooth haggling," 'cuz you don't stop until you draw blood!

Flinging my cheetah pocketbook like I have more in it than a tube of S.N.A.P.S. lipstick and a disposable instant camera, I stroll into the bookstore.

There are three tricks of the bargaining trade: 1. You gotta act *très* nonchalant, like you really don't want the thing in the first place; 2. After you ask how much the thing costs, act very surprised that it's so expensive; and 3. After the salesperson tells you the price, look at other stuff, so they can stew that they lost the sale, then wait for them to quote a lower price.

"Bonjour," I say to the salesperson, a blond woman with bifocal glasses crooked on her nose. The rest of my crew stands around, ogling the movie star photos, while I do my thing.

"How much is the Josephine Baker poster in the window?" I say, stifling a yawn, then casually glance at a picture of some "creepy crawler" named Adam Ant.

"Five thousand," says the saleslady, giving me a look like I can't afford it!

Don't come for me, Missy, I want to snap, but I stay cool as a fan. "Oh," I simply respond, stifling another yawn, then continue looking at Mr. Ant's photo.

It seems like five years have gone by before the saleslady says, "You know, it's a vintage 1936 photo, but I can give it to you for four thousand."

"Oh, that's fabbie-poo, darling. Let me think about it—I'm off to an auction. Toodles!"

I have to run out of the store, because I'm about to lose it, and I can see my crew trailing fast behind me.

"Bravo, darling!" Mom says, clapping her

hands when I get outside, then the rest of my crew joins in. "That was a performance worthy of an Academy Award for Best Actress in a Bookstore!"

I curtsy and prance in front of everyone till we get to the next corner. Then I catch a glimpse of my mom, looking back toward the store, with a real sad look on her face, like she wants that poster in the worst way, but can't afford to get it. Again, I get that guilty pang in my stomach. I wish *I* could shell out the duckets myself for the poster.

"Which way to Aunt Kizzy's?" I ask, changing the subject to get her mind off her misery.

"Just follow the smell of corn bread!" Aqua heckles, darting forward to the quaint little door to Aunt Kizzy's Back Porch.

Although there are no movie stars at Aunt Kizzy's, there really is an Aunt Kizzy, and she makes "the best macaroni and cheese and candied yams outside of Texas," claims Aqua after we've finished our fabbie-poo lunch.

"Just don't barf it up!" quips Chuchie as we're leaving. Everybody waves good-bye to us, too. La La Land is *definitely* a lot friendlier than New York. It must be all the sun and fresh air.

"Y'all Cheetah Girls come back and see us real soon," Aunt Kizzy says in her booming voice, waving at us from the BBQ grill. "Good luck with the showcase, too. If y'all sing as good as you eat ribs, you'll be riding around in a Bentley in no time!"

"Yo. We're getting a Jaguar, right?" Dorinda asks, looking up at me.

"Nope. A cheetah-mobile," I quip back, grabbing a toothpick from the stand by the door. I can feel all the gunk stuck in between my braces.

"That was good food in the 'hood!" I say, smacking my lips, imitating the twins. Then I get busy poking at the shredded rib with the toothpick. "Look, Chuchie, even the toothpicks are red."

"And so is the back of your skirt, *Mamacita*!" Chuchie shrieks, grabbing my arm and pulling me aside.

"Say it ain't true, blue!" I reply without thinking, because I'm turning red. "Is it my period?"

"*Sí, Mamacita.* What else!" Chuchie says, looking at me like I'm a dodo.

Chuchie knows how much I *hate* getting my period. That's why it catches me by surprise half the time. I just wish it would *pouf* and go away, and come back another day!

I run inside to the ladies' room, to check out the disaster. Walking by the table where we ate, I can't help but look at the chair I sat in. *Omigod,* there is a little red stain on the plastic cushion!

I hightail it to the bathroom, and go inside a stall, where no one can see how embarrassed I am. I sit on the toilet seat and put my face in my hands. *How could I get my period today?*

Chuchie stands on the next toilet seat, leans over the top of the stall, and peers down at me. "You okay, Bubbles?"

"No! I'm not okay, Chuchie. Get a stupid sanitary napkin or something."

Mom always tells me to carry tampons with me, and I don't listen, because I *hate* getting my period!

This time, Chuchie hands me a sanitary napkin under the stall. "You owe me a quarter," she says, giggling.

"Chuchie, you'd better sit your *butt* down before I make change!"

"Don't be mad at me," she exclaims. "Here, you can put my sweater around your skirt. Nobody is gonna notice, *está bien?"*

"Chuchie, I'm just so embarrassed, I'm never leaving this stall!"

"*Está bien*, Bubbles. I'll stay here with you all night, but let me go tell everybody not to wait for us."

"Very funny, bunny," I tell Chuchie. Then I start giggling, too. It is mad funny, in a pathetic sort of way. "Don't you hate being a girl?" I ask her.

"No," Chuchie giggles.

"I don't know why the sight of blood never bothers you, Chuchie, when you're generally such a squeam queen."

I sigh, then get up and leave the stall. "Let's go see Hollywood," I tell Chanel.

When we go back outside, Mom is patiently waiting. "It's okay now, darling?"

"Yeah, I guess," I mumble, then sulk. I'm so glad she doesn't bother me about it.

"Ms. Dorothea, that food was really good," Aqua says, trying to deflect from my misery, no doubt. That's one thing I can say about the twins—they're always looking out.

"I'm glad you enjoyed it, 'cuz that's gonna be the last meal you eat before you 'sing for your supper!'" Mom quips.

I know she's teasing. Dorinda doesn't get it, though, and she looks at Mom like she's already hungry! I wink at Dorinda, and instant relief floods her adorable little face. That's what I love about Do'—she can always go with the flow.

"Mom, is the record company paying for *everything*?" I ask, as we walk to the next destination on our supa-packed itinerary. I feel really uncomfortable with Chuchie's sweater tied around my waist—and I *hate* wearing sanitary napkins.

"No, darling. It's not *all* paid for. They paid for our airfare, car service to and from the airport in both cities, and hotel suites. The rest comes out of your Cheetah Girl retirement fund!"

I swallow hard. That was not the answer I was hoping to get. It means Mom and Dad are paying for all our little extras—and when the Cheetah Girls get together, those little extras can add up in a hurry!

"I hope we have something to retire *from*," Chuchie says wistfully.

"I heard that," Dorinda retorts, then grabs Mom's arm. "You don't think we're gonna end up on the chitlin' circuit, or something like that, do you?"

"Not as long as I'm your manager—what you do after you fire me is your business!" Mom says, and laughs out loud.

I grab Do' Re Mi by the arm, and we start skipping down the street together. Do' Re Mi doesn't really understand that the Cheetah Girls are down for the 'do—together, forever, whatever makes us clever.

There's no reason why she should she settle for being a backup dancer—yet—but I know where she's coming from, and one day, I hope she realizes where *we're* going.

"Hey, Cheetah Girls!"

That voice again! I freeze in my tracks, waving weakly as the brothers from the Big Apple come toward us. "Hey, Stak, hey, Chedda," I say, trying to smile. But my hands go straight to Chuchie's sweater, which is wrapped around my bloody dress. If they see me like that, I'll never get over it, I swear! Why is it Stak Chedda always shows up when tragedy strikes?

"How's the video comin'?" Stak asks.

"Video?" I repeat dumbly. Then I remember my fib-eroni. "Oh, that—it's goin' with the flow," I say.

"That's dope," Chedda says.

"Hey," Stak adds, "maybe we could be in your video—you know, put in a little cameo appearance or something!"

"Yeah!" Chedda says. "We wouldn't even charge y'all!"

"Uh, no!" I say, looking at Dorinda for some help.

"Our contract says 'no other artists,'" she says, pulling one out of the air. "It's an 'exclusive.'"

"Exclusive, huh?" Stak says, looking at us suspiciously. "I never heard of that . . . are you sure y'all just don't wanna share the spotlight? Afraid we might outshine the Cheetah Girls? Tony the Tiger wouldn't mind."

"Yeah, right," I say, flossing. "That'll be the day, when y'all outshine the Cheetah Girls!"

"We did it at the Apollo," Chedda reminds us with a big grin.

"Now, now, brotha," Stak says, motioning for him to back off. "Let's be gentlemen. These ladies got a good groove. Just 'cuz we won, that don't mean they ain't got it going on."

"I hear that," Chedda says, backing off.

"How's it going with your uncle *Dudley*?" I ask, trying to turn the attention away from us. Looking down the street, I see that Mom and Chuchie, along with the Walker twins, are admiring yet another window display. Why don't they get over here and help us?!

"Uncle Dudley's just fine, ain't he, Chedda?" Stak says, poking his brother.

"Uh, yeah—yeah!" Chedda says. "He's feelin' much better."

"Was he sick?" Dorinda says.

"Yeah—didn't we tell you?" Stak says, stumbling a little. "He's okay now, though. And he's gonna back us with some serious loot."

One thing I can tell is a fib-eroni when I hear one. Trust me. There ain't no Uncle Dudley, and something is fishy in La La Land.

"Uh, we gotta go," Stak says, pulling Chedda away from us. "See y'all around, Cheetah Girls!"

Funny how they decided to hightail it out of there, right when we started talking about *them,* not *us.* But I don't have time to worry about Stak Chedda, and what they're doin' out here in the City of Angels. Right now, I'd better find out where my "Road Runner" mom is dragging us.

"Where we going next, Momsy-poo?" I ask as she and the rest of my crew catch up to us.

"First, we're going to Mann's Chinese Theater."

"What's that?" Dorinda asks curiously.

"There's where they have all those famous footprints in cement," Mom says.

"Oh. Can we go where they have all the stars on the sidewalk?" Dorinda asks.

"That would be the Hollywood Walk of Fame, which is our next stop right after Mann's," Mom answers. "Then we can shoot over to Wilshire Boulevard, and head to the La Brea Tar Pits Museum, to check out some saber-toothed tigers."

"Real ones?" Aqua asks, her eyes getting wide.

"No, darling, we're the only *real* attraction the jiggy jungle has to offer today," Mom says, chuckling. "These tigers are built around bones of the ones who fell in the tar pits millions of years ago. They're truly fierce-looking. But if you don't want to go there, we can skip right to the Grave Line Tours and see the Grim Reaper. I'm sure you'll dig that!"

"Yeah!" Aqua and Angie scream in unison. "We love you, Ms. Dorothea!"

"Well, okay, I guess Hollywood's lions, tigers, and bears won't be graced with our growl power this trip," Mom says, amused. "Besides, there's nothing like a creepy cemetery for catching some peace and quiet!"

We snicker our skulls off taking in the sights, and later, the trendy boutiques on Melrose Avenue. Melrose is like the Soho section of Manny-hanny—also known as Manhattan, to the tons of tourists who swarm there *every* minute. Do' Re Mi and I don't mention our little meeting with Stak Chedda to the rest of our crew. No sense worrying them over nothing, right?

"When do we get to go shopping?" Chuchie asks, half-jokingly. *"Estoy nervosa.* I'm getting the willies about tomorrow night. I need to shop."

Poor Chuchie. Her shopping days were nipped in the bud when she ran up Auntie

Juanita's charge card. Now she has to work part-time in Mom's store till she pays off the credit card bill. Mom says Chuchie's really good at dealing with customers, too. I'm not surprised. Chuchie is really sweet—when she isn't getting on my nerves, that is.

Right as we're passing the candy-striped awning for Canine to the Stars Pooch Parlor, we get a good glimpse of how the pampered poochy half lives in La La Land. Dogs with rhinestone collars are perched in chairs, getting their paws done.

"Ooh, look at her bou bou fon fon!" exclaims Chanel, as this lady with a bleached white bouffant strolls to the entrance of the parlor with her poodle in tow.

"Oooh, excuse me, miss, can I pet him?" I ask the lady politely.

"It's a she," the lady says snobbily.

"Oh, I'm sorry, what's her name?"

"Godzilla," the lady says with a straight face. "If you don't mind, we're in a hurry, because she's late for her paw-dicure."

"Oh, I'm sorry!" I exclaim, then watch her go inside. "Wow, did you see how tight her face was?"

"Darling, that's because she's had so many facelifts, she'd scare a mummy out of his tomb!" Mom says.

"Word," chuckles Do' Re Mi.

I'm only half listening, because I'm too busy staring into the parlor window, looking at the dope display of poochy collars they've got there. "I'm definitely angling to get my paws on that cheetah-studded collar," I whisper to Chuchie. "Toto will love it!"

Toto is my boo-boo. He's also like my brother. *Mom's* baby. She named the store after him: Toto in New York. And of course, she named *him* after Toto in *The Wizard of Oz.*

Mom gives us a look like, "Oh, go on inside."

That's all the permission we need. The five of us hightail it into the store, to ogle the pets and stuff.

"That collar you like is thirty dollars!" exclaims Aqua, fingering the price tag.

"So?" I hiss, forking over the exact amount to the saleslady. "I just won't eat lunch at school for . . . well, forever."

"Okay, Miss Galleria," Angie says, giving me a look, like "We'll see."

"My prize pooch is gonna look like a prince,"

I announce. Then I turn to Chuchie and say, "I miss Toto so much. Do you think I should get him that turkey costume for Thanksgiving?"

"No—he'll think it's a drumstick, and try to eat it," Chuchie says, fiddling with the new cheetah shades she just bought on the cheap up the block. "Ooh, look at these stick-on rhinestones. I'm gonna buy these!"

"Those are for pooches?" I ask Chuchie.

"*Yo no sé,* but I'm gonna get them."

"Do you think this is the right size collar for Toto?" I ask, holding up the cheetah collar.

"It looks kinda big," Chuchie says, shrugging. "But don't worry. If it doesn't fit him, *I'll* wear it!"

Leave it to Chuchie. "Yeah, I bet you would!"

I put the boot-i-ful cheetah collar in my cheetah purse, and swing it all the way to our next stop, which turns out to be an unplanned one.

We're passing by this building, and the sign outside says "Frederick's of Hollywood Museum." I look in the windows, and let out a little scream—it's a *bra museum!*

"We've gotta go in there!" I say, excited. I've been wearing bras since I was eleven years old (unlike Chuchie), but these in the window are really dope ones!

"Oh, great, I get to feel flat-chested," Chuchie moans, as we look at the displays of bras, some of which have cups that look like torpedos ready for takeoff.

"Oh, those are 'old school' ones," I explain to Do' Re Mi, who is fascinated with them all. She's so small, she doesn't have to wear a bra either.

Finally Mom makes us leave, and we go to a thousand more places, looking at stars' footprints in cement, stars on the pavement, and finally, real stars in the nighttime sky. Finally, we start seeing stars swimming before our eyes, because we're so tired. Still, we're happy and excited. We've had one of the best days of our lives, tooling around the incredible City of Angels.

We go back to the hotel, eat a fancy room service dinner, and spend the rest of the evening lounging around our boot-i-ful suites.

After our baths, Do' Re Mi and I flop down on the bed we're sharing. We lay there in the dark, with Mom snoring in the next bed, but neither of us is sleeping. Not yet. I know we're both thinking about tomorrow night, nervous and excited at the same time.

"This is all like a dream, isn't it?" Do' Re Mi giggles, nuzzling her head into the incredibly soft pillow.

"It sure is," I say softly. "I just hope I'm not about to wake up and find out this is another *Nightmare on Elm Street*!"

Chapter 5

Today is our "last chance, last dance" to frolic in the Royal Rooster swimming pool. At three o'clock, we have to go do a sound check at the Tinkerbell Lounge, then come back to the hotel and get dolled up and down for the 'do, which starts at seven o'clock.

A "sound check" is exactly what it sounds like. The stage manager of the venue adjusts the lights and audio to the right levels, to make sure that everything is "on the money" for the real performance.

If the microphone situation isn't right, you could get onstage and sound like a hyena singing an aria. We're all kinda nervous about it, because the other performers in the showcase will be at the sound check, too. And we know they'll be checking us out while we're checking out the competition, if you know what I'm saying.

My crew and I are hanging out at the deep end of the swimming pool, to stay away from all the noisy kids in the wading area.

Mom is lying on a beach chair, because she doesn't like to go swimming—lest her wig, she says, "does the float." Aqua and Angie are playing water volleyball, and doing flips in the water. Do' Re Mi is ferociously swimming laps, like an Olympic swimmer. Meanwhile, I'm flapping my feet like Flipper, and annoying Chuchie, who is lying nearby on a Royal Rooster inflatable float, preening behind her new cheetah sunglasses and bikini. Chuchie has an "outie" belly button, like I do, and she does look *très* cute in her bikini, because she has long legs and a flat tummy.

"*Párate,* Bubbles!" Chuchie moans in Spanish, putting her hands over her face to keep from getting her glasses wet. I know she doesn't like to get her braids wet, either, because if she doesn't dry them right, they get a serious case of mildew!

"Do you think there'll be a lot of peeps at the showcase?" Chuchie asks me. I can tell she's getting nervous, but I'm just trying to chill.

"Sí, Mamacita," I say, spurting water from my mouth. "I don't think they'd fly us out here just to sit with Captain Hook and a snook!"

If fairy tales do come true, then the Tinkerbell Lounge on Sunset Boulevard is the place. We're half an hour early for the sound check, so we stand outside under the lounge's silver awning, pressing our faces against the glass window to see inside.

"Everything is silver and shiny—even the big disco balls hanging from the ceiling," Do' Re Mi reports, like she's an interior decorator or something. "Even the couches are sprinkled in stardust!"

As we wait, I start humming verses from the song I wrote, "Welcome to the Glitter-dome," because it reminds me of why I have dreams, and how we got here. My crew joins in and sings along just for fun:

"Twinkle-dinkles, near or far,
stop the madness and be a star
Take your seat on the Ferris wheel,
and strap yourself in for the man of steel.

Welcome to the Glitterdome
It's any place you call home.

Give me props, I'll give you cash,
then show you where my sparkles are stashed.

Glitter, glitter. Don't be bitter!
Glitter, glitter. Don't be bitter!
Glitter, glitter. Don't be bitter!"

We're so caught up in our reverie that we don't notice someone else has arrived at the scene of the rhyme—but I would recognize *that* voice in a dark alley from the bottom of a Dumpster truck.

"Yo, Cheetah Girls—Tony the Tiger let you out the house again?" It is none other than Stak Jackson, stepping out of a black Town Car and onto the sidewalk, with his brother, Chedda, trailing right behind him.

"It's like *déjà vu,*" Chuchie gasps under her breath.

"*This* isn't *déjà vu*, Chuchie," I hiss, "'cuz this nightmare already happened—and I can't believe it's happening *again*!" How could two rappers—unknown to the world as Stak Chedda—strike twice like lightning? Where is Cheetah Girl justice when you need it?

Bracing myself for a showdown, I put my hand up over my left eye as if I'm shielding myself from the sun. "Yellow satin—it's a little bright for 'Sunset' Boulevard, don't you think?"

"Not as bright as you, Cheetah Girl," Stak Jackson says, grinning from ear to ear. "You in the showcase, too?"

"Um, yeah," I say, then sigh because my last shred of hope that the bumbling bozos were here as a janitorial team has just been yanked away. "I just made that up about the music video," I admit.

"Oho!" Stak says, laughing it up. "Afraid Stak Chedda gonna come away with the cheese again?" He and Chedda high-five it, grinning from ear to ear.

"How's your uncle Dudley?" I ask, smirking, 'cuz I know there *ain't* no Uncle Dudley.

"Uh, well," Stak says sheepishly.

"I thought so!" I floss. "I guess he's resting in peace!"

Now it's the Cheetah Girls' turn to high-five it!

Luckily for all of us, just then a tall man with a lopsided buzz cut steps to the entrance of the Tinkerbell Lounge and asks, "Are you the Cheetah Girls?"

"Yes," I reply, speaking for the group like I usually do. It's one of my problems sometimes, but all in all, I'm not sorry I'm that way—a lot of times, it helps to just get it out, know what I'm sayin'?

"I'm Paul Pett, the showcase coordinator," he says, extending his hand to shake mine. I like his professional groove already.

"Hi, I'm Mrs. Garibaldi," Mom says, extending her hand now, like it's a delicate lily waiting to be sniffed for its aromatic qualities. "Remember, we spoke on the phone?"

"And we're Stak Chedda," breaks in Chedda Jackson, like someone asked him. "An A and R guy from your label peeped us at Club Twice as Nice in the Bronx, remember?"

"Ah, yes," says Mr. Pett, trying to be "twice as nice," I guess.

Aqua gives me that fabulous Walker twins puzzled expression, but Do' Re Mi steps to the plate with a piece of the puzzle. "What's an A and R guy?"

"Oh, that's the record company executive who signs an artist and is responsible for groom-their career, so to speak," Mr. Pett explains.

"Yeah. It means 'artist and repertoire,'" Chedda explains, like he's got it going on in the "knowledge department."

I want to scream, "Don't try it." But for this once, I keep my mouth shut.

"Mr. Brumble, the club manager, should be here any minute," Mr. Pett explains to us all, then turns to Mom and asks, "Did you have a good flight?"

"Yes," Mom says, telling a fib-eroni. I guess she figures there's no need to go into all the gory, snory details about the night we spent in the Twilight Zone.

"Ah, here's Mr. Brumble now," Mr. Pett says, stepping aside to let the club manager open the lounge. Mr. Brumble is wearing a black eye patch, and has two gold hoops in each ear and long wavy hair.

"Mr. Pett, how many acts will be performing

in the showcase?" Mom asks, taking off her cheetah shades as we go inside. Even though it's daytime, and bright and sunny outside, it's still kinda dark inside the Tinkerbell Lounge—making it seem even more spooky and sparkly.

Humph, I think as Stak Chedda follows us inside. What Mom should've really asked Mr. Pett is how many *animal* acts will be performing in the showcase. How else did these two bumbling bozos make it onto the same bill as *we* did?

"Let's see, we have the rap group CMG—the Cash Money Girls. Um, the male quartet—Got 2 Be Real 4 You. The Beehives—which is a hot rock group from Boston. Stak Chedda —whom we're billing as an alternative rap duo. And, let's see, the Toads—a country-western group who already have a *huge* following in their hometown, Nashville."

What does Mr. Pett mean by *alternative* rap group? I wonder. An alternative to what—death by a wack-attack?

"Mrs. Garibaldi," Mr. Pett asks Mom, smiling. "Since some of the bands aren't here yet, do you mind if your girls do their sound check first? That way, you can get on out of here and have some time to yourselves before tonight."

"It works for me," Mom says, motioning for us to go on the oval stage. Right in front of the silver tinsel strip dividers are a cool set of drums, keyboards, and bass stands. That would be so dope, if we had instruments like that! You know, just banging on some keyboards and singing songs would be off the hook!

Maybe one day. For now, Mom hands Mr. Pett the instrumental tracks we use for the songs "Wanna-be Stars in the Jiggy Jungle," "Shop in the Name of Love," and "More Pounce to the Ounce."

Mr. Brumble tells us to stand right in the center of the stage, and floods us with a glaring spotlight, then softens it to a pinkish hue, with shooting stars bouncing off the stage.

"That's dope," Do' Re Mi says, smiling.

After the lights are adjusted, the tracks are cued up, and we sing a few bars of each song to cue the audio.

At this point, I'm relieved we don't have to stay and wait for the rest of the groups. In particular, I can't wait to bounce from the Stak Chedda situation.

"Why are those hyenas grinning at us?" I whine to Chuchie as we leave the Tinkerbell Lounge and head outside. Behind us, I can feel Stak and Chedda Jackson staring at us, thinking they got us right where they want us. "We're not their next Happy Meal, okay?" The next thing I know, we're in "hyena territory," as Mom would say.

"Yo, check it, Cheetah Girls," I hear Stak Jackson yell from behind us. I turn around, and see that he's poking his head out the front door of the club. Now he pushes the door all the way open and comes over to where we're standing on the sidewalk.

"I just wanted to say, we—me and my brother—was feeling you at the Apollo. And, um, we're sorry the situation had to go down like that. Um, you know what I'm saying?" Stak says, smiling and showing his pointy fangs.

"Yeah," I pipe up, rolling my eyes to the bright blue sky. "You shouldn't have won, *we* should've!"

"Um, well, I wasn't exactly going there, you

know what I'm saying, but, yeah, you Cheetah Girls had something to say—maybe in another situation, you coulda smoked us," Stak says humbly.

"For true," I reply, not knowing quite how to handle a hyena when he's being so nice. That was the last thing I expected him to say, tell you the truth.

"That was *real* nice of you to come out here and tell us that, 'cuz you know we were heartbroken *we* didn't win," Aqua pipes up.

Who asked her? Doesn't she have a new church hymn to learn right about now?

"We'll see who's got the situation locked up later," Do' Re Mi says, egging Stak on the dis tip.

"I heard that," he chuckles, adjusting his baseball cap like the sun is in his eyes.

"Where are you from?" Chuchie asks him.

"The boogie-down Bronx. That's where we call home," Stak says, and suddenly his pointy fangs don't look so pointy. "Yo, I'd better bounce, though, 'cuz we still gotta do our sound check—so I'll catch you later, awright?"

"Whatever makes you clever!" I say, then call after him the one question I want answered. "Yo, Stak. How did you and your brother get the hookup for this New Talent Showcase?"

"One of my boys told us some peeps from Def Duck Records would be rollin' up into Twice As Nice on the Grand Concourse, on open mike night with DJ Sweet, so we signed up. And, well you know, we freaked it," Stak says, flexing his hookup.

"Freaked it, huh?" I say, trying to stop smiling. "That's how I would describe, um, what you do."

"Well, you know, that's Stak Chedda—and nobody does it better," Stak says, trying to hide his hyena fangs and flex some more by winking at me. "How'd you Cheetah Girls get the hookup, yo?"

"Kahlua Alexander told Def Duck about us, and they flew us out here," I say, flexing back hard.

"You got it like that?" Stak asks, his eyes opening wide.

"Yeah, but *we'd* better bounce now," I say. I yawn, then put on my cheetah shades. "See ya—and I wouldn't wanna be ya!"

Stak shakes his head at me, still grinning,

then goes back inside. Instantly, we all crack up laughing.

"You're so *wrong*, Bubbles!" Chuchie says, giving me a Cheetah Girls handshake as we walk a few feet to the Town Car, where Mom is already waiting for us.

"Dag on, these rap groups seem to get all the breaks," Aqua says as we settle down in the backseat. "Galleria—you don't think it's gonna turn into Nightmare on Sunset Boulevard, do you?" she asks, chuckling nervously.

The rest of my crew gives me a look like, "Oh, no, not again," but I'm not having it.

"We've already paid the Boogie Man in full," I tell them, pushing my hair from my face, 'cuz it's gotten a little stuck from the sweat. "We're here, aren't we? This time around, we'll *see* who gets to put some duckets in the bucket!"

Chapter 6

Now, it's time to do or die. Back in our adjoining suites, Mom sews some extra stitches on the tail of Do' Re Mi's cheetah costume. I've been soaking my stained cheetah blouse, and now I'm blow-drying it. The stain seems to have come out, thank gooseness!

Chuchie has had a dope idea for our hair. "We can stick the rhinestones I bought all over our hair with a little Wacky Glue!" she explains excitedly.

"I'm down," says Do' Re Mi.

"Me, too," I giggle. "After the strobe lights hit the rhinestones, and we dazzle them with our skills, we'll be the stars of this showcase, paws down!"

That's Chuchie, always hatching new hairdos. "This Wacky Glue stuff isn't gonna be hard to get out of our hair later, is it, Chuchie?" I ask. But when she doesn't answer, I figure she knows what she's doing, and I let it go.

"Lemme see yours," I ask the twins when they finish. Even on their smooth bobs, the rhinestones give mad sparkles.

"You hooked us up, Chuchie!" I yell happily.

We grab the garment bags with our costumes, and head downstairs to the lobby. "At least the Tinkerbell Lounge has a dressing room, so we can change there," I quip. "We're making a rapid climb up the food chain, Cheetah Girls!"

"I heard that," Aqua says, smiling ear to ear. "I can't believe how this all turned around! I mean, we lost the Apollo contest, and now just a couple weeks later, we're here in La La Land, performing for a record company! It's like out of a movie!"

"It sure is," Angie agrees.

"And I hope we get to see this movie again and again, *está bien?*" giggles Chuchie. She has put about fifty rhinestones into her braids, and they are shimmering all over the place, making her look like Sistarella, the fairy princess.

"All you need is a magic wand," I chide my make-believe sister. Then I give her a big, tight hug.

Without Chuchie, I could never do any of this. Actually, without the five of us, I don't even think we'd have gotten this far. Sure, Chuchie and I used to dream, but nothing ever happened until we met Dorinda, then Angie and Aqua.

When we roll up to the front of the Tinkerbell Lounge in our Town Car limo, I can't believe how beautiful the lounge looks, now that the sun has set on Sunset Boulevard. My whole body is tingling with excitement, and I can't help holding Chuchie's hand as we go inside.

"Hello, ladies. You're in the showcase, right?" says a hostess wearing a silver sparkly jumpsuit with a silver mesh net tutu.

"Yes, darling, they are," Mom says, pointing to us.

"Come right this way," the hostess says, showing off a sparkly smile.

I just love the peeps in La La Land. They're so *friendly,* and it seems like everybody here wants to be a shining star.

"You can put your stuff in your available dressing room," says the hostess, "and make yourselves at home. As talent, you're entitled to complimentary beverages and entrees of your choice. We've got a spread laid out downstairs in the club, but you can eat right in your dressing rooms. Just give your order to Raven—she's the waitress responsible for talent—and she'll bring your order to the dressing room when it's ready."

The hostess points to a pretty girl wearing a costume with silver wings. "Mr. Pett will be in to see you soon. Have a wonderful showcase!" She leaves us, and now it's time to find our dressing room.

"What a difference from the Apollo, huh?" I say to Chuchie, as we walk past a silver tinsel curtain and into the back hallway. "Am I tripping, or did she say our dressing room?"

"*Mamacita,* for once you're not 'lipping,' 'cuz *mira,* there it is!" Chuchie excitedly points to a dressing room, which has a piece of white paper with *our* name taped on its door!

I open the door excitedly, like one of those game show contestants anxious to see if we won the grand prize or just a booby prize.

Chuchie switches on the light, and I like what I see. "Lip, lip, hooray, we are definitely in the house!" I gasp, fingering all the lipsticks, powders, and oodles of beauty products and stuff on the big vanity table, surrounded by a supa-big vanity mirror with supa-big lightbulbs!

"Miz Aquanette, we didn't forget about you, 'cuz I got something for you, girlina," I start teasing Aqua, and moving sideways so she can't see what I'm hiding behind my back.

"What is it, Miss Galleria?" Aqua asks, giving me that look, like "I'm ready for Freddy, yo."

Whipping out a big aerosol can of Aqua Net hair spray, I act like I'm gonna spritz her, cornering her against the wall and making *Pssst* noises. "Did your mom name you after this little can of hair spray?" I ask, laying on the Southern accent.

"No, Miss Galleria, I really don't think she even heard of it!" Aqua pipes up. "I know Angie got her name from our great grandmother, Anginetta."

"Anginetta, I'm gonna let her—" I sing, making up rhymes like I always do.

"Shhh!" Mom hisses, and moves to the door, because all of a sudden, there is lots of giggling and noise in the hallway. As she opens our dressing room door, we all gather around to get a whiff of the action, and quickly realize that the other acts have arrived.

The center of the commotion is none other than a posse of girls wearing chain-link mini dresses featuring dollar bills.

"I guess we know who that is," Aqua chuckles, 'cuz she favors ducket designs, too — like the dollar bill decals on her tips.

Making their way to the dressing room with their name tacked to the door—"Cash Money Girls"—one of the girls turns around and says, "Sorry, we hope we didn't disturb you."

"Not at all, darling," Mom says. "We just got here ourselves. I'm Ms. Dorothea, manager of the Cheetah Girls."

"Hi—we're CMG—the Cash Money Girls. I'm Georgia Washington," the platinum blonde says.

Then the one with the upswept braids turns and says, "I'm Benjamina Franklin."

The one with the Miss Piggy eyelashes says, "Hi, I'm Abrahamma Lincoln."

"We'll check you later," I say, smiling, as we pile back into our dressing room.

"Their dresses are too short," Mom snips, then closes the door behind us.

"I'll bet you they're from out here," I offer as an explanation. All the girls out here seem to dress more "summery," if you know what I'm sayin'—probably all year round, I guess.

"You think those were their *real* names?" Angie asks.

"Lincoln, Washington, Franklin—duh!" Do' Re Mi says, exasperated. "Angie, those are 'dead presidents'—as in duckets, m-o-n-e-y, get it?"

"I get it," Angie says, kinda embarrassed, but shrugging it off. Then she mumbles, "After all, Benjamin Franklin wasn't a *real* president."

"Look at who *finally* cracked open her history book in school," quips Do' Re Mi.

"At least they had a theme—unlike those bozos Stak Chedda," I grumble.

"We're not going to wear the masks today, right?" Do' Re Mi asks as she changes into her cheetah costume.

"No, I don't think that's the move. Right, Mom?" I turn and ask.

"No, let 'em see what they're getting. I think you should put that glitter stuff around your eyes. You know, 'Cheetah Girls don't litter, they glitter!'" Mom says, chuckling.

"I *like* that, *Madrina!*" Chuchie exclaims.

"That's dope, Mom," I exclaim, then whip out my notebook and write it down. "Cheetah Girls don't litter, they glitter."

That gives me another dope idea: "You know, if—I mean, *when*—we get a record deal," I say, correcting myself, "we should come up with our own Cheetah Girls Credo that we could put inside the CD or something."

"You mean, like the Cheetah Girls Rules we have?" Do' Re Mi asks.

"Yeah, sort of, but more like things we believe in—with some flava," I add.

"Word. That's dope," Do' Re Mi chuckles.

"'Cheetah Girls don't litter, they glitter,'" I repeat out loud, staring at the scribbled page in my spotted, furry Kitty Kat notebook, which is like my personal Bible and secret diary mixed together—and it's for my eyes only.

"Should I wear my hair down?" I ask, smoothing down the fuzz that's growing by the minute. "Maybe I shoulda gotten another weave?"

"I guess you would've, if you had weave money," Mom snips at me.

All of a sudden, I feel my eyes fill up with tears. Mom would never snip at me like that if she wasn't mad at me about something! I was right, I suddenly realize. It's my fault Mom and Dad have to work so hard.

"Oh, weava, don't ever leava!" Chuchie giggles, not realizing what's going on with me. "I like it wild like that, Bubbles. That's the real you."

"I like it straight," I say, frowning to hide my real feelings. "I look like a Chia Pet with all this hair."

"Bubbles, if you put it up now, you're gonna mess up the rhinestones!" Chuchie says, exasperated because, I guess, I'm freaking out. "*Párate!* Now you're making me *nervosa.*"

"Okay, girlinas, calm down. It's time to growl, not *howl,*" my mom interrupts.

We start chuckling. Mom *is* mad funny, even though she is too bossy sometimes. Besides, I've got to give it to her—she didn't say anything when I stained my skirt yesterday at lunch. Of course, that's probably because she's tired of yelling at me to carry tampons.

Which reminds me. Taking out a tampon from my cheetah backpack, I make a mad rush to the ladies' room. "Come with me, Chuchie. That's all I would need is to start *leaking* onstage!"

Chuchie giggles, and follows me out the dressing room door. Four guys in big cowboy hats and boots, and bright red plaid shirts, are rambling our way. They smile at us, and I almost wave with the hand that's holding the tampon. Luckily, Chuchie pokes me, and I pull it back in time. "Oopsy, doopsy," I giggle, then say, "Howdy."

"Howdy, ladies. Those costumes are mighty pretty!" the tallest guy says.

Cheez whiz, they have a drawl even bigger than Aqua and Angie's!

"Who are you?" asks nosy Chuchie.

"The Toads," says the tall guy wearing the hundred-gallon cowboy hat. "And y'all?"

"We're the Cheetah Girls!" I say, recovering from my tampon embarrassment.

"We're y'all from?"

"Manny-hanny!" Chuchie says, then giggles. "And you?"

"Nashville, Tennessee—and believe me, we're *real* glad to be here!"

In the bathroom, I can't stop giggling about our little encounter with the lonesome cowboys. Then, I suddenly get another idea, "Maybe we should get cheetah cowboy hats, and do a 'jig'—I mean a gig—at a rodeo!"

"Where *is* the rodeo?" Chuchie asks, standing outside my stall, holding the door because the latch is broken.

"I don't know. Down South somewhere, no? Let's ask the goody two-shoe twins!"

"*Qué hora es?* What time is it?" Chuchie asks, sounding nervous.

"Six o'clock. Time is moving so slow today," I say, feeling cold and chilly, even though the weather is so perfect in La La Land. I always get cold feet when I'm nervous.

"Feel my hands," I say to Chuchie, grabbing her hand. "I'm cold as a mummy. You are too, Chuchie."

When we get back to the dressing room, Mr. Pett is waiting for us. "Oh, we're sorry to keep you waiting!" I exclaim.

"No, that's fine. I just got here. Is everything okay, ladies?" Mr. Pett asks, like he really wants to know. Nobody asked us *anything* at the Apollo—even when we were boo-hooing like babies backstage after we lost. That's 'cuz they didn't give a hoot *how* we felt.

"Everything is fabulous," Mom volunteers. "Do you have our place in the lineup yet?"

"Yes, I do," Mr. Pett says, flipping a page on his clipboard. Then, smiling at us, he adds hesitantly, "We want you to go on first. Now, I know that isn't the ideal spot in a showcase, but —"

"But *nothing*!" Mom encounters, interrupting Mr. Pett with a smile. Then she blurts out, "We'd have better luck facing a *firing* squad than being forced to warm up a bunch of suits."

"I know. I know, Mrs. Garibaldi, but in order to provide diversity for the showcase, we're breaking up the talent by, um, musical genre," Mr. Pett says, stammering. He sounds like a used-car salesman trying to unload a broken-down hooptie.

"Well, let me break this down for you by, um, 'growl power' genre," Mom says, very politely, so I know she's mad. "We're *not* going on first."

"Okay, lemme see what I can do," Mr. Pett says, taking a handkerchief out of his suit pocket and wiping the sweat from his forehead.

Mom picks up the menu and starts looking at

it. I know better than to say anything, so I just throw Chuchie a look, then start fiddling with my hair and staring in the vanity mirror.

"Ms. Dorothea, what did you mean by a bunch of 'suits'?" Aqua asks Mom, breaking the silence. She *would* ask a question now.

"That's what you call record industry executives—exactly who will sitting there judging us, if we go out there howling instead of growling," Mom explains, exasperated. "Let some other poor prey be led to slaughter first!"

"I know that's right!" Aqua responds.

A few minutes later, a very nervous Mr. Pett knocks on our dressing room door, and announces the new—and improved—lineup.

"Mrs. Garibaldi, I pulled a few strings, and the Cheetah Girls will go on right after the Beehives. That'll be a nice segue from rock to, um—"

"*Global groove,*" Mom says, to help Mr. Pett from flexing fowl and calling our music by some wack name.

"Yes, that's right, 'global groove,'" he says, breaking into a nervous smile. "Anyway. After the Cheetah Girls, we'll segue into the country-western genre with the Toads, so it'll work out perfectly after all."

"I agree with you, Mr. Pett. That sounds like a *purr-fect* lineup," Mom says, to keep Mr. Pett from "cracking face" any further. "Just give us our cue when it's time to *growl*!"

That's my mom. Sometimes, she bosses me around, it's true. But I'll tell you what—when it's time to stick up for your own, there's nobody like Ms. Dorothea.

Chapter 7

As show time at the Tinkerbell Lounge approaches, we nervously open the door to our dressing room so we can keep our ear to the action, if you know what I'm saying.

Standing in the doorway, with Do' Re Mi scrunched against me, we catch four girls with supa-powdered faces, black-lipsticked pouts, and the highest "bou bou fon fons" we've ever seen, hovering together at the far end of the hallway.

"Those must be the Beehives," Do' Re Mi whispers to me.

I nod my head, like "No kidding." One thing is for sure, the Beehives must be causing quite a buzz in Boston with *that* look.

It seems a lot of girl groups have four girls — just like Karma's Children in Houston, where the twins are from, or the Honeydews. I'm glad the Cheetah Girls are "representin'" with five strong, you know what I'm saying?

All of a sudden, the audience starts clapping, which usually means that an announcer has stepped onto the stage. Sure enough, the announcer's voice booms into the microphone, trying to hype the crowd.

Do' Re Mi and I tiptoe a little farther out into the hallway, just to hear what he says. Thank gooseness Mom got us out of first place in the frying pan—we woulda sizzled for sure!

As we stand there, just a few feet from the stage, my heart starts to *thumpa, thumpa* up a storm, and I start getting so nervous I can't breathe. This is it, I tell myself. Tonight's the night we get a record contract, and start making beaucoup duckets, or else our faces are cracked.

That would be a total nightmare, I say to myself. My mom would probably have to quit managing us and get busy again in her shop. Dorinda would probably go off and dance with Mo' Money Monique and leave the group. It would be the beginning of the end for the Cheetah Girls!

No! I can't let it happen! It's all up to me, I think. I've got to come through this time!

"What's he saying?" Do' Re Mi asks quietly.

"I can't hear," I respond, but that's probably because my heart is pounding so *loud*.

The Beehive girls start shuffling closer to the tinsel curtain divider. Then, on cue, they rush out onto the stage.

We scurry back into the dressing room, because it's time to do our Cheetah Girls prayer. We do our prayer before every performance. I think it gives us good luck and, more important, reminds all five of us that we're in this together—*forever.*

After we finish doing the prayer, we take a few deep breaths. I can feel my hands tingling.

Just clear your mind and concentrate on your breathing, I tell myself. I can hear our vocal coach Drinka Champagne's voice in my mind, telling us what to do before we "hit that stage."

We all look at one another and smile. Mom looks up from eating her plate of linguini, and gives me a big smile, too.

The lyrics from the Beehives' performance

waft all the way down the hallway: "Sting me with your love/Or I'll fly away like a dove. . . ."

I look at Chuchie, and she knows what I'm thinking. "I've never heard that song before," she says, shrugging her shoulders.

Whenever we hear singers, we're always trying to figure out if they're doing "covers" or singing original songs. It seems like a lot of groups sing other artists' material. But we're not going out like that. Mom says I have a gift for writing songs. But I just feel like, why should I put duckets in someone else's bucket by singing *their* songs, when I can sing my own, you know what I'm saying?

All of a sudden, Mr. Pett appears at our door, and Mom jumps up. "It's show time!" she announces, taking the words right out of Mr. Pett's mouth.

We all hold one another's hands, and follow her lead into the hallway. Judging by the clapping, there are a lot of peeps in the house.

At this very moment, I'm not worried about anything—not about Stak Chedda, not about duckets, fame, or fortune. Right now, at this second, I don't even care if we get a record deal. I just can't *believe* the Cheetah Girls are in the house—in La La Land! Somebody throw poppy dust on me, *pleez*!

After the announcer introduces us, Mom throws us a kiss, and pushes us gently from behind the tinsel curtain. I look quickly at the crowd, and breathe a sigh of relief as we line up across the stage and wait for our audio cue.

The crowd is not so scary-looking or anything. They don't look like *our* kind of peeps, but at least they look like regular people. I mean they're not giving off any Darth Vader vibes or anything.

Mom says that the A&R peeps from Def Duck Records are definitely in the house, checking us out. That gives me the shivers again, but thank gooseness, I'm saved by the beat. The bass-heavy tracks we use to sing our song, "Wanna-be Stars in the Jiggy Jungle" crank up loud over the sound system.

Omigod, I hope that doesn't drown out our vocals! I suddenly think. I start goospitating, but there is no time left for a visit to freak city. We already did an audio check, and the engineer wouldn't have set the audio level that high if the mike level didn't match, I tell myself.

Then I start grooving on automatic, doing our dance steps, waiting for the vocal cue, counting to myself, One, two, three:

"Some people walk with a panther
or strike a buffalo stance
that makes you wanna dance

Other people flip the script
on the day of the jackal
that'll make you cackle."

By the time we get to the refrain—*"The jiggy jiggy jungle! The jiggy jiggy jungle!"*—I can tell the crowd is feeling our global groove. It's not exactly like it was on Halloween, when we performed at the Cheetah-Rama for our fellow Kats and Kittys, but this crowd is definitely *feeling* us, too.

When we do our second song, "Shop in the Name of Love," I throw Chuchie a quick little smile, and from her eyes I can tell we're on the same "weave length." I wrote the song just for her, after she got busted running up Auntie Juanita's charge card. Juanita has not been *feeling* Chanel lately, but I know Chuchie's trying real hard to make up for everything, 'cuz she let us all down.

When the intro beat pipes up, we get ready for our "fierce pose"—placing our arms over our heads—which is a fly move Do' Re Mi thought up. Then we spin around, and break into the lyrics:

"Polo or solo
Gucci or Pucci
Prada or nada
Is the way I wanna live."

By the time we take our bow, I'm so psyched, I'm not even nervous anymore—I just wish we could sing *one more song*! But that's the deal-io, yo, with showcases: you only get a teeny-weeny slice of the performing pie. I can't wait till we're serving it piping hot till our spots drop!

Because Mr. Pett told us to leave the stage quickly after we perform, we don't really get to take in all the applause. Mom is waiting for us behind the tinsel divider, and she hugs me and Do' Re Mi when we get inside the dressing room.

"Were we dope?" Do' Re Mi asks, looking up at Mom.

"Better than that," she says, smiling with pride. "One of you is fierce enough, but *five* of you? I hope the world is ready for Freddy, okay?"

"What about me, *Madrina?"* Chuchie whines, moving in to Mom for a hug, too. Mom is Chuchie's godmother, and sometimes Chanel really milks it for points.

"Prada or *nada*!" Mom sings, imitating Chuchie, and we really start giggling, because Mom's singing voice is a cross between the Tin Man's and Minnie Mouse caught in a tropical rainstorm. *Squeak, squeak, squeak!*

Finally, I can relax and eat, so I pig out on Mom's leftover linguini with white clam sauce. "Yum yum for my tum tum," I hum as I chomp away.

Raven, our waitress, knocks at the door. "Can I get you girls anything else?" she asks.

"Yeah—a record deal!" Chuchie giggles.

"Just some more soda," Mom pipes up.

"I'll be right back," Raven says, smiling. Lifting both arms over her head, she waves them, fluttering her fingers.

Aqua and Angie give each other a look. "Her name is Raven," Aqua says.

"Yeah, and she just 'spread her wings,'" Angie adds. "You think High Priestess Abala was right?"

"I sure hope so," Aqua says.

"Well, I don't know about any predictions of the future, but I do know I like her costume," Mom says after Raven leaves. "Which reminds me, girlinas—don't change from your costumes yet. Mr. Pett says that after the last act has performed in the showcase, Deejay Captain Hook will start spinning records, and we can go back into the performing area and mingle with the executives, and have complimentary cocktails."

"Complimentary cocktails, that sounds dope!" chuckles Do' Re Mi.

"Well, some sounds are deceiving, darling, because in your case, cocktails are synonymous with *Coca-Cola*!" Mom warns her.

"I know," giggles Do' Re Mi, "but you know what I'm saying."

"Yes, darling, and I'm not playing. We're just gonna go out there to sashay and parlay till it's payday!"

We all laugh at Mom's rhyme, then run back into the hallway to hear the Toads perform.

"They sound more like frogs!" Chuchie quips, after we listen for a few minutes.

"When you grow up down South, you learn to *love* country-western music," chuckles Aqua.

"Yeah, well I think it sounds too *twangy,*" I moan. "Like they should be performing in a square dance or something."

"Yeah, and those country-western acts are twanging all the way to the bank," Mom quips. "Did you know that, after rap music, country music artists sell the most records?"

I see Mom is taking her job as our manager very seriously. These days, she reads *Billboard* magazine, and she's even got bookworm Do' Re Mi reading the "trades," as she calls them.

"Well, I know there are a lot of corny people out there, so I'm not surprised that they buy corny records," Chuchie says, picking at the rhinestones on one of her braids.

"Stop that, Chuchie," I scold her, moving her hand from her hair.

"Chanel, those rhinestones were sparkling up a storm under the lights," Mom says, pleased.

"I know, *Madrina,* but I'm not so sure they come off!"

"Well, we don't have to find out right now," I scold her again, as she tries to touch her hair on the sneak-a-roni tip.

Twirling in the vanity chair, I ask wistfully, "Don't you just love getting Hollywood-ized?"

"Yeah," Chuchie says. "I can't wait till we come back out here *otra vez.*"

"I guess you will, when you have come-back-out-here money for plane tickets," Mom quips, packing some of our stuff back into her cheetah vanity case.

Man, I hope we get a record deal out of this. For Mom's sake more than mine, so she can stop working my nerves!

Do' Re Mi motions for me to come listen at the door. "They're on."

I know exactly who she's talking about. Those "dead president" divettes-in-training are finally dropping a few pennies worth of rhymes onstage. Angie comes running back into the dressing room to tell us, "Those heffas are really throwing money onstage!"

She would be impressed. "Don't worry, Angie, you *know* they aren't *real duckets*!"

"I know, but maybe *we* should do something like that," Angie says sheepishly.

"Yeah, we could throw stuffed cheetahs at the audience," I say with a smirk. "And with our luck, it would hit the vice president of the record company on the head and give him a concussion."

"You're a mess, Galleria," Angie says, chuckling sweetly.

Sometimes I can't understand why the twins are so *nice*, but they just are. "CMG's definitely got some flava," I mumble, while listening to the group's set.

Mom hates their outfits, so she doesn't even get up to hear their performance. Angie runs back by the tinsel divider, while CMG keep the flow going:

"Yeah, we rool with Lincoln,
What are you thinkin'?
But it's all about the Benjamins.
Baby, not maybe, just mighty, awrighty!"

Chuchie and I look at each other, like "all right, they got rhymes." The executives are obviously feeling CMG, too, because the Cash Money Girls get a mad round of applause.

"I'll bet you they get a record deal," Do' Re Mi says seriously. "It seems like record companies are always willing to bank on a few rhymes, yo."

"I know that's right," Aqua pipes up. "Yeah, they're good, though."

"Hey, this isn't a competition, remember," I remind my crew. "It's not like, if some other group gets a contract, we don't—it's not like the Amateur Hour at the Apollo, where only one group wins."

From the relieved looks on the faces of my crew, I know I've said the right thing. Thank gooseness!

We all hover by the door now, to wait and see CMG come back to their dressing room. When they do pass, we congratulate them

"Where are you from?" Chuchie asks the girl who calls herself Abrahamma Lincoln.

"We're from Oakland," Abrahamma says, smiling at Chuchie.

"Where's that?" Chuchie says giggling.

"It's up north," Abrahamma responds, amused.

"North *where*?" Chuchie asks again, with no shame in her game.

"Oh, y'all ain't from around here. It'sup in northern California," Abrahamma says, chuckling.

"Chanel falls asleep in geography class," I offer, because I'm so embarrassed for her. Even *I* know where Oakland is!

"How old are y'all?" Abrahamma asks me, because it's obvious we're still in school. They look like they're probably twenty-two or something.

"We're freshmen in high school," I say, flossing.

"Oh, well, y'all are real cute. I love your costumes! Did you make them?" Benjamina Franklin pipes up.

"No, my—um, our manager made them," I say quietly, changing my mind about saying "my mom."

The announcer introduces Stak Chedda, so we all get quiet and listen. "How is it they *always* get to go on last?" I hiss to Chuchie.

"Oh, do you know them?" Benjamina Franklin asks me surprised.

"No," I say, because I'm definitely not telling *them* we got dis-missed at the Apollo Amateur Contest, and they won instead. "We, um, performed with them once before."

"Word. Where?" Benjamina asks me. Cheez whiz, she's like a dog with a bone, she just won't leave it alone.

"We performed with them at the Apollo Thee-ayter," Aqua volunteers. Now I'm back to hating the goody two-shoe twins *again.*

"Word. Y'all performed at the Apollo?" Abrahamma asks, like she's impressed, but not quite.

Now I *really* want to do an "abracadabra."

"We just performed in the Amateur Hour Contest," I say, my voice squeaking because I feel embarrassed now.

"Oh, yeah, that's right, we was talking to the taller one earlier—Stak Jackson—and he told us they *won* the Amateur Hour Contest," Abrahamma says, a flicker of recognition on her face.

Suddenly, the tinsel dividers fling open, and my worst nightmare starts walking *our* way, with their hands in the air like they just don't care. "*Ayiight!*" Stak Jackson says, slapping his brother, Chedda, a high five, like they definitely rocked it to the doggy bone.

I guess they did, but I'm not feeling the bumbling bozos, after the way they dissed us at the Apollo. I don't care how nice Stak's trying to be to me now.

"I'm not *feeling* him," I mumble to Chuchie, rolling my eyes to the ceiling.

"You wuz off the hook, Cheetah Girls!" Stak says on the way to his dressing room, which is at the other end of the hallway. Thank gooseness the Tinkerbell Lounge is big—just like everywhere in La La Land.

"You were, too," I hear myself saying, even as I'm gritting my teeth.

Chuchie giggles. She thinks it's so funny, 'cuz bozos always seem to like *me.*

Mom comes to the doorway. "It's show time, girlitas—*again.*"

We know that means we're supposed to go back out into the performing area, and be *really really* nice to all the peeps we meet. This is real important, see—it's not enough to be talented, as my mom's been telling us—you have to go out there and "shmooze" with the "suits" if you want to nail down a record deal. And do I ever want to nail one down, right to the floor!

Deejay Captain Hook comes up to the mike. He tells us he'll be spinning on the "wheels of steel," and to sit back and dig the sounds.

"He's funny," I laugh to Do' Re Mi. "The peeps out here are kinda cooler, more laid-back than peeps in Manny-hanny. I definitely like it!"

A man in a white linen suit comes up to Mom, and extends his hand. "Hi, Mrs. Garibaldi. I'm Tom Isaaks from the A and R department at Def Duck."

Mom is really nice to him, which is surprising, because she usually gaspitates at people who wear white after Labor Day, but I guess she knows what time it is. It's definitely time to sashay and parlay!

Do' Re Mi and I back away, so Mom is free to flow. I keep an eye on her, as I accept congratulations from members of the other acts, and from people who were in the house. Everyone says they loved us, and they're wearing big, goofy smiles, so I know they either mean what they're sayin', or they're just playing.

But part of my attention is always on Mom and Mr. Isaaks, 'cuz he's the one we're after right now. There are other A and R guys here, no doubt, but this one came up to mom first thing.

As I'm standin' there, I catch Stak and Chedda Jackson high-fiving it across the floor from me, nodding their bozo heads up and down like they're all that and a bag of chips. I'm thinking I want to go over there and find out what all the hip-hoppin's about, but they beat me to the punch.

"Yo, Cheetah Girls," Stak greets me and Dorinda. "What the deal-io, yo?"

"Chillin', chillin'," I say, trying to act cool like a jewel. But what Stak says now sends a real chill up and down my spine.

"Looks like Stak Chedda got us a record deal!" Stak nods, flashing his pointy-toothed grin like he's sitting on a million duckets.

"For true?" Dorinda asks, her jaw dropping. "Man, that was fast!"

"We don't waste no time, waitin' for no dime!" Chedda gloats. "Y'all got any interest goin'?" Stak asks me.

"My mo . . . our manager's talkin' with the A and R dude right now," I say. And from the look of things, it's getting serious between Mr. Isaaks and my mom. Their smiles have vanished, and now it looks like he's explaining the ins and outs of things to her.

"Well, good luck, yo," Stak says, giving us a little hand salute. "Y'all really rocked the house. You deserve a deal, just like us." He and Chedda move off toward the cocktail bar. I guess they're old enough for cocktails, come to think of it.

Now Mom comes up to us. "Where are the other girls?" she asks. We look around for them. Chuchie is flirting with some hunky executive in a shiny suit and mirror shades. The twins are by the food spread, talking to the Beehives, their mouths full of food.

Do' Re Mi and I go round them up, and we huddle with my mom. "Well, Cheetah Girls, Mr. Isaaks is interested in signing the Cheetah Girls to a contract. . . ."

We whoop and holler for a minute, hugging one another and crying tears of joy.

My mom tries to stop the party. "Whoa, now, wait a minute, I haven't finished telling you the whole story!" We calm down, and she continues. "He says, though, that it's not all up to him. He's got to play our tape for some higher-up executives, and try to convince them he's right about signing the Cheetah Girls."

"So, what does that mean?" Chuchie asks,

the smile fading from her face.

"It means, we probably won't know anything for a while, and we're just gonna have to be patient and wait."

"How long is a while?" Dorinda asks.

"He says it could be a few weeks before he knows anything, but that we can call and check in if we start getting anxious, and he'll give us an update of his progress."

"A few weeks!" Aqua gasps. "Dag on, that's like forever!"

"Yeah!" Angie echoes. "How come it's got to take so long?"

"Well, apparently, not everyone was here who had to hear you girls sing," Mom explains.

"But Stak Chedda got an offer just now!" Dorinda breaks in, saying just what I was about to say.

"Well," Moms shrugs, "I don't know . . . maybe the executives from the Alternative Rap division were all here or something."

"Yeah," Chuchie says, "and maybe they're just better than us."

"Put a lid on it, Miss Cuchifrito!" I say. "If we have to wait, we'll just wait."

My crew all agrees, and we get together and

do a Cheetah Girls cheer. But inside, I feel like I'm falling apart. A few weeks! Can the Cheetah Girls even hang together that long? Without any gigs, with no duckets coming in, Dorinda might find some other paying gig performing and Auntie Juanita may yank Chuchie out of the group. And what if "a few weeks" becomes a few months? What if we don't get the deal, after all that waiting? It'll be the end for us, I just know it!

Chapter 8

If I thought the drama we had trying to get to L.A. for the Def Duck Records showcase was like being in the Twilight Zone, then I was wrong. Flying *back* from Cali on the overnight "red-eye," to go to school in the Big Apple the next day with a cold, a splitting headache, *and* a bad attitude, is *really* what it feels like to be in the Twilight Zone.

Right this minute, Chuchie and I are walking to our lockers after third period. I can't even walk fast, because it makes my head hurt more. What a roller-coaster ride our life is! "I can't believe just yesterday, we were living large in Cali, and today we're goospitating about a stupid math exam," I moan to Chuchie, who is lost in her own Telemundo channel, as usual.

I *hate* math, and would rather have someone stick my eyelashes together with Wacky Glue than have to figure out another algebra equation! "Equate this—squared times x to the fourth power equals nonsense!" I moan to Chuchie. She's even worse in math, except, of course, when it comes to adding up how much money she can spend *shopping*!

"You don't think this looks stupid, do you, Chuchie?" I ask, fingering the cheetah dog collar I'm wearing around my neck. It's a good thing the collar fit *me,* because it sure didn't fit Toto. When I got home and tried to put it around my boo-boo's neck, it was too big for him by an L.A. mile. *What was I thinking when I bought it?*

"No, *Mamacita.* It looks dope. I wish I had one," she whines wistfully. "*Pero,* I can't believe you don't know what size Toto is by now."

"I was delirious, okay, Chuchie?" I groan.

Chuchie changes the subject. "Do you think you passed the math exam?"

"I don't know, did you?" I snap back, then shove some books into my locker. "Thank gooseness it's lunchtime, 'cuz I'm fading pronto. I feel like I'm about to fall on my face."

"Well, you *are,* 'cuz here comes the Red Snapper and Mackerel," Chuchie giggles sarcastico.

Derek Ulysses Hambone, a.k.a. "DUH," is the biggest pain, but I try to be nice to him, because his mother is a very good customer at Mom's boutique. "I don't understand why all the bozos like me," I mumble under my breath.

Derek is in our face now. "Yo, Cheetah Girl. We missed you yesterday. I heard you was getting busy in Cali. That true? Kahlua Alexander hooked you up with a showcase?"

Derek is sucking on a lollipop that makes him look like a—well, like a Red Snapper. Mackerel Johnson, "his boy," is bopping around as usual, and grinning at Chuchie like he's waiting for a visit from the tooth fairy.

"Yeah, it's true," I mumble, trying to smile at Derek. He is wearing a red sweat suit, with the Johnny BeDown logo up the side of the pants and across the top in jumbo-size black letters. How tick-tacky.

"That's dope, you got it like that. Did you get a record deal yet?" Mackerel cuts in, amping up his hyper moves.

"We don't know *anything* yet," I reply, irritated 'cuz I don't wanna think about it, and I don't want them to know we've got it like that—waiting nervously like hungry cubs. "We just did it for the experience, you know what I'm saying?"

"Yeah, I hear you, Cheetah Girls. I know y'all gonna blow up one day, and I'll be like Batman—*bam*! Right there by your side when it goes down," Derek heckles, grinning at me with that awful gold tooth in front. "You should let me be your manager, yo."

"Thank gooseness, we already have a manager," I smirk back at him.

Suddenly, the Red Snapper is staring at my neck like he's a vampire, which gives me the chillies. "Yo, check that choker around your neck. That is *dope.*"

Chuchie starts giggling, and I'm really gonna whack her if she tells Derek that the choker around my neck is really a *dog* collar!

"Thanks. I bought it in Cali," I say, telling only half a fib-eroni.

"Too bad, 'cuz I'd like one of those. I'm gonna be modeling in this fashion show at my mom's church, and it would look dope with the designs I'll be wearing—cheetah stuff like you like," Derek explains, flossing.

"Well, it's not too bad, because we *make* them, too," I say, smirking at my quick comeback.

"Word? Well then *make* me one—you know I'm good for the duckets," the Red Snapper says, pulling out a wad of money from his deep-sea pockets.

"Awright, but you got to pay to play—tomorrow," I retort.

"How much? Oh—make the choker a little wider, too," Derek says, waving the hand in which he's flossing his duckets.

"For you, Derek, we'll let you slide for, um, twenty," I say, thinking off the top of my head.

"Okay, bet. Later, Cheetah Girl."

Chuchie and I hightail it outside to wait for Do' Re Mi, then walk toward Mo' Betta Burger on Eighth Avenue.

"You won't believe what Bubbles just did!" Chuchie says, grabbing Do' Re Mi's arm and filling her in on my entrepreneurial moves.

Mom would be so proud of me, I think. Instead of waiting around for a record deal to appear, I'm goin' out there and makin' things happen in the duckets department. One way or another, I'm gonna show her and my dad that I can make my own payday. I'm not some spoiled brat, like Derek Hambone!

"If Derek would just give up on the gold rush, maybe I could at least look at him without *puking*," I mumble to Do' Re Mi.

"Word. I hear that."

Suddenly, I get a great idea. "Maybe I should send him an anonymous letter, telling him he wouldn't look like such a wack attack if he took out that gold tooth. You think that's a dope idea?" I suggest to my crew.

"Nope, 'cuz he'll know it's from you," Do' Re Mi says. She's smart, so I listen to her.

"Yeah, you're right. Too bad."

"You really gonna make him a cheetah choker?" Do' Re Mi asks, squinching up her nose as we walk inside Mo' Betta, order some burgers, and chill at a table.

"Yup," I counter. I'm getting my chomp-a-roni on with a mushroom burger, when I suddenly get another fabbie-poo idea! "I'm even gonna put my nickname for Derek on his choker, in silver letters—*scemo*!"

Chuchie almost chokes on her burger, giggling.

LaRonda, one of the girls in my math class, walks by our table. "What y'all up to?" she asks, checking out our mischief moves.

"Nothing," I reply, trying not to choke.

"The math test was hard, yo, wasn't it?" LaRonda groans, still standing by our table.

"Yeah, it sure was," I respond.

LaRonda looks at me, then gives me the same vampire look that Derek did. "That choker is dope. Where'd you get that, yo?" she asks, excited.

"Actually, I, um, I mean, we make them," I say, telling one whole fib-eroni this time. If I'm gonna sell one to the Red Snapper, I might as well sell one to LaRonda while I'm at it, you know what I'm saying? "We've got a few different styles. I, um, we could make you one like this."

"That sounds cool. How much you selling 'em for?" LaRonda asks, panting like a puppy for our product.

"Ten dollars," I say, charging LaRonda a cheaper price than the Red Snapper, since she's cool.

"Word. Can you make me one?"

"Yup. I'll bring it to school tomorrow," I tell her proudly. "But you know you got to pay to play, yo?"

"Ayiight. Don't worry, Galleria, I'll have the money. Just bring me the choker," LaRonda says, then walks away.

"LaRonda—you want me to make you one with your name on it?"

"Word—you can do that?" she turns and asks, her eyes brightening even wider.

"Yup—that's a done deal-io, yo," I say, flossing, and go back to eating my burger. LaRonda smiles, and goes to the counter to order.

All of a sudden, I notice my headache is gone, and my mind is ka-chinging like a cash register as I talk real fast to my crew. "The three of us can go after school today to the garment district, and buy the leather strips, some metal letters, snap closures, Wacky Glue, and we're in the house—in business, yo!"

Chuchie and Do' Re Mi look at me like "Bubbles is trouble." I see I'm gonna have to convince my crew to be down with the new endeavor that will make us clever.

I take a deep breath, like Drinka taught us to do, then do my wheela-deala. "Look. We can sit around here, waiting for Def Duck or some other record company to give us a record deal. And that is definitely cool, yo, but we're Cheetah Girls, and we've got the skills to pay the bills, so why not parlay and sashay?"

Chuchie starts giggling and gets excited. I can see she's finally hopping on the choo-choo train. After all, she needs money a lot worse than I do so she can pay her mother back all the money she charged on her credit card! "Maybe we should make some chokers so we can sell them at Kats and Kittys!" she suggests hopefully.

"Word, that would be dope," Do' Re Mi chimes in. I know Do' can use some duckets worse than any of us—her "family" has got no money at all, once they get done feeding all those foster kids and paying the rent. "We could even try to sell them to stores—I mean, um, little stores, anyway," Do' Re Mi adds, wincing, then shrugs her teeny-weeny shoulders.

"You think *Madrina* would sell some for us in the store?" Chuchie asks me.

"You're the one who works there part-time, so *you'd* better ask her," I chuckle. "I'm not asking Mom for any more favors. She does enough for us."

"It's not a favor, flava—it's about bizness," Do' Re Mi says, smirking and sipping on her Coke.

"Well, I think we should make up a few chokers first, then try to sell them to a boutique or something, and only then ask Mom. She'll *have* to say yes, if someone else buys them from us first, right?" I say, whipping out my Kitty Kat notebook to make some notes. "Okay, we'll make, um, eight chokers that say—what?"

"Why 'what'?" Do' Re Mi asks.

"Not *what*, silly—but what should it say?"

"Oh. How about 'Growl Power'?" Do' Re Mi says, looking at us for approval.

"Do' Re Mi, you are so *money*—that's dope!" I say, getting really excited. "Okay, we make five chokers for ourselves, so we'll wear them all the time. Kind of like a walking advertisement for our product. Then we'll make three more, which we'll try to sell. Then one more for Snapper—that says, scemo. One for LaRonda. Should we make LaRonda's name with just capital letters, or small ones, too?"

"LaRonda. I like it with capital and small letters. Maybe we should get gold and silver letters, though," Do' Re Mi suggests.

"Yeah, that's cool. Okay, after school, let's get busy, 'cuz it's time to put some duckets in the bucket!"

Chapter 9

I'm so glad the twins have finally talked their father into letting them get a cell phone. Of course, he wouldn't spring for a Miss Wiggy StarWac, like Chuchie and I have, but at least it works, even if it's a "no name" model.

"Angie, meet us at Pig in the Poke on Fortieth Street," I tell the twins, so they can get in on the choker action, too. Because Chuchie, Do' Re Mi, and I are students at Fashion Industries High, we have a special discount card that we can use at any store if we're buying stuff for school—like sewing, design, or pattern-making supplies. So our best bet is to go buy supplies for the chokers in the heart of the garment district—which is pretty much below Forty-second Street, near Times Square.

LaGuardia Peforming Arts High School is just a hop and skip down from there on the #1 train, so it only takes Aqua and Angie twenty minutes to get hooked up with us.

"That skirt is cute," Chuchie says to Aqua. The twins actually do look cute today. I mean, it's not how *we* three dress, but they're starting to get their own style groove, which is cool. They have on matching black-and-white-checked mini-skirts, with black sweaters and flats. Dressing alike is not just a cheetah thing—it's a twin thing, too.

"Did you tell High Priestess Abala about that waitress, Raven, we met?" I ask, kinda half-jokingly.

High Priestess Abala and the twins' dad are getting a little too serious too fast for Aqua and Angie's taste. Of course, it doesn't help that Abala probably goes to work on a broomstick, too! I think she's definitely part of some kooky coven, you know what I'm saying?

"Yes," Angie pipes up, "and she says that that's the sign we were looking for, and that it means the record deal is *ours*!"

"Don't you think that's going a little far, Aqua?" Do' Re Mi snips. "I mean, all Raven did was serve us some linguini and Cokes and that's no joke!" Do' Re Mi is definitely the only one in our crew with her feet planted firmly on the ground.

"You know, I could definitely use some of High Priestess Abala's Vampire Brew right about now, yo," I say, smirking. "I still cannot believe we were sitting up there in your living room that time, sipping witches' brew with a coven of psychos, just because Abala told us it would bring us good luck at the Apollo!"

"I know you're right. You remember that noise me and Angie heard in our bedroom closet before we left for Hollywooood?" Aqua says, using her drawl to do a vowel stretch.

"Yeah. Did you catch Mr. Teddy-Poodly doing the tango while eating a mango?" I riff. High Priestess Abala had given us all shoe boxes filled with teddy bear eyes and noses, poodle tails, and rabbit whiskers. She said we were supposed to put them in our closets, and not open them, if we wanted to rock the house at the Apollo. Wack advice, if you ask me.

"No, Galleria, the only thing we caught in

that closet was a mouse—that's what I'm trying to tell you!" Aqua says, bursting out laughing.

"Hold up," I say wincing. "You mean to tell us that all that shaking and baking you said was going on in the closet had nothing to do with the shoe boxes? It was a *mouse* in the house?"

"Yes, ma'am. That's right," Angie says, nodding.

We all give each other a look like we're gonna have to keep this Abala situation on the down low, 'cuz something is definitely not right.

"Were you scared?" Do' Re Mi asks.

"Well—" Aqua hems and haws.

"Stop faking that you're not quaking, Aqua!" I blurt out.

"All right, Galleria. We wuz scared to death! You happy now. I didn't sleep but forty winks, ain't that right, Angie?"

"That's right," Angie says, nodding, and eating her sandwich from a cellophane bag. "Even Porgy and Bess wuz scared!" Porgy and Bess are the twins' pet guinea pigs.

We crack up all the way to Poly and Esther

Fabrics, on Fortieth Street between Seventh and Eighth avenues—that's where Mom says they sell the cheapest cheetah suede prints this side of the jiggy jungle.

Of course, I'm in charge of bargaining and negotiations. "I'm getting really good at this," I humph, as I approach the counter. "I don't stop till the price drops!"

Well, I guess I've met my match today, because Mr. Poly isn't having any eyelash fluttering today. "Miss, you either pay the twenty-two dollars a yard, or you take your business somewhere else!"

"Okay, okay," I say, giving in, and reluctantly taking the exact sum out of my cheetah wallet. We're chipping in ten duckets each to float our Cheetah Girls choker escapades, so the rest of my crew is paying for the other accoutrements.

"Next time, I'd better negotiate with his better half—Mrs. Esther," I mumble as we leave the store, on our way to buy the silver and gold metal letters.

"Have any of your rhinestones come out of your braids yet?" I turn and ask Chuchie.

"No, *Mamacita*. Not one," Chuchie says,

touching her braids and showing me how stuck they are. "I bet you they stay in until I get my braids taken out next week."

"I can't believe you're taking your braids out, just 'cuz Kahlua did, Chuchie," I mutter. "You're such a copycat."

"What happened?" Chuchie stutters, then changes the subject, which is her favorite escape tactic. "If the Wacky Glue lasted this long on our hair, the metal letters will really stick to the suede fabric."

"You sure, Chuchie?" I ask casually.

"Sí. Estoy seguro."

"Okay, then let's roll with it," I say. In the sewing supplies store, we get busy, grabbing a big bottle of the supa-gluey stuff, two bags of metal letters, and a bag of snap closures to secure the chokers.

"Did you get enough letter G's?" Do' Re Mi asks.

"Enough to start a Growl Power war!" I heckle back. Then I dial my Dad at the Toto in New York factory, to tell him we're on our way.

"Ciao, Daddy," I say, throwing him a kiss over the phone before I hang up. "We're lucky duckies he's gonna let us use the equipment at

the factory," I tell my crew, "'cuz I really didn't want to ask Mom to help us." I'm definitely satisfied with our escapade so far. "Mom's gonna be so psyched when she sees the chokers."

"How come she doesn't make Toto in New York accessories for the store?" Do' Re Mi asks.

"She only makes cheetah backpacks and stuff like that. She says it's easier to buy bags and jewelry than make them, 'cuz it's less manufacturing headaches," I explain. "But we're in this for more than headaches, girlitas. I have a feeling we're gonna be churning these chokers out by the baker's dozen!"

Dad supervises a staff of five at the Toto in New York . . . Fun in Diva Sizes factory, where all the clothes for Mom's store are cut and sewn, then dropped off to the *très* trendy boutique in Soho that my parents own.

"Cara, cara, and *cara!"* Dad says, kissing Do' Re Mi, Chuchie, and me on both cheeks. That's an Italian thing, you know what I'm saying? When Angie and Aqua come out of the bathroom, dad does the same thing to them. The

twins *really* like my Dad, 'cuz he's so much cooler than their stuffy pops. Cool as a fan, that's my dad.

Dad sets us up at the drafting table, where we lay out the suede fabric to cut it into strips for the chokers. *"Posso ayudarte?"* Dad asks me in Italian, our private language, but I don't want his help. I want to make these chokers with my crew.

"Dad—go do your work. We're chillin', *va bene?"* I say, mixing Italian and English together the way I always do when I'm talking to him.

"Chill then, *cara,"* Dad says, making fun of me.

He looks really tired lately, but I don't say anything about the bags under his eyes. I wish my parents didn't have to work so hard, and I can't wait till I can pay for everything, so they can just go to Stromboli, or Giglio, or any one of the cazillion beautiful island resorts in Italy that they love so much. I'm gonna buy them a house there, too, so they can retire when they're old. I'm gonna show people that I'm not so spoiled as they think.

Since Do' Re Mi is the most skilled among

us, she gets to cut the strips of suede. Angie, Aqua, Chuchie, and I use the T-square rulers to draw perfect lines for Do' Re Mi to cut along.

"How many strips did we get from a yard?" Chuchie asks after we've finished cutting up the yard of suede.

"Thirty-six strips, which we can cut in half to make seventy-two chokers," Do' Re Mi explains proudly. "We don't have to make all of them now, though."

"Awright!" I shriek. "We're in business!"

Next, we have to sew two suede strips together on Dad's industrial machine. Gracias, who has been a seamstress at the factory for ten years, sets us up at the machine, which is used for sewing leather, suede, and heavy coating fabrics like fake fur, which Mom uses a lot for fierce Toto in New York designs.

The gadget that intrigues Do' Re Mi most, though, is the machine used for applying the snap closures.

"Ouch!" I wince, as I try to clamp down on a snap I've placed over a strip of suede. Dad comes running over, and I get really annoyed at him.

"Va bene, va bene. Do it yourself," Dad says,

finally letting me have my way and leaving us alone.

The most fun we have is gluing the metal letters on the chokers.

I'm anxious to get my grubby little paws on our first "product." "It's not dry yet," protests Do' Re Mi, as I pick one up to try it on.

"Okay, okay," I say, getting impatient. Mom says that I'm too impatient, but I don't agree with her. If you want things to happen, you gotta move, you gotta groove, you know what I'm saying?

"Okay, *now* groove, Galleria," Do' Re Mi says, handing me one of the chokers.

"This is *so* dope," I exclaim, holding the cheetah choker in my hand like it's a baby or something. "Girlinas, we're ready for Freddy!"

Now I'm ready to talk to Dad, and I go running over to show him the chokers that we made all by ourselves, without his help.

"Que bella, cara!" he exclaims, and I think he really means it, even though Dad is down with whatever I do.

Dad insists that I wrap the Cheetah Girls chokers in tissue paper, then put them in a cheetah-print Toto in New York shopping bag. "You must always make a *bella* presentation when you want to sell something," he explains to me.

"Va bene, Dad," I giggle. I guess it won't kill me to accept the shopping bag and tissue papers.

We are all so amped by our first business venture that on the way home, I get another fabbie-poo idea. "Let's give our chokers a 'test run,'" I suggest to my crew. "Nobody knows us in Brooklyn, right? Why not try to sell a choker to one of the boutiques here?"

"I'm down," Do' Re Mi blurts out.

"That sounds good," Aqua seconds.

Chuchie just shrugs her shoulders and giggles as we walk down the block from Dad's factory to Fulton Street. The Toto in New York factory is only five blocks from the coolest shopping area in Brooklyn, known as Fort Greene, which is supposed to be like a black Soho or something. Kinda "boho," you know what I'm saying?

"How 'bout this one?" I turn and ask Do' Re Mi. We have stopped in front of a colorful boutique called Kumba, which has all these African caftans and safari-looking stuff in the window.

"I don't know. You think they'd go for it?"

Angie says. "It looks like the kinda stuff High Priestess Abala wears."

"For true," I say, "and she would look so much doper if she was wearing one of these!" I'm so excited by all this, I'm just dying to go in *anywhere* and see what they say.

"Está bien. Let's try it," Chuchie says, heaving a sigh.

The first thing I notice when we walk inside of Kumba is a really strong aroma. "What's that smell?" I whisper to Chuchie, who has the keenest nose for scents.

"Mija, it's just incense," Chuchie says, smiling. We stand looking around, kinda nervous, because everything looks really expensive. A dark man, wearing a turban on his head and a caftan piled with lots of beads, comes from behind a beaded divider.

"I'm Mr. Kumba. Can I help you?" he asks politely.

"Yes, sir, um, we're the Cheetah Girls, and we make chokers that we'd like to show you," I respond politely.

"Oh. Show me what you've got," Mr. Kumba says curiously. "What do you mean by 'Cheetah Girls?'"

"Oh, we're a singing group and, um, we do lots of other things," I try to explain.

"We go to Fashion Industries High School, too," Do' Re Mi says proudly. "I major in Fashion Design."

I guess she's trying to impress Mr. Kumba with the fact that we aren't just a bunch of kids, probably because everyone thinks she is so much younger than she really is.

Suddenly nervous, I pull the Cheetah Girls chokers out of the Toto in New York shopping bag, and lay them carefully on the glass display case. Glancing inside the case, I notice all sorts of African-looking beads made into necklaces, bracelets, and earrings. Aqua's right, this is the kind of stuff that High Priestess Abala would wear. Maybe after Mr. Kumba places an order, we can go bragging to her, and she'll come shopping here!

"What are these?" Mr. Kumba asks, holding up one of the chokers.

"They're, um, chokers," I explain calmly, but I can feel my face getting warm.

"They look like *dog collars,* if you ask me," Mr. Kumba retorts, then puts on his glasses to read the metal letters on the choker. 'Growl Power'—that sounds like something for dogs. What is this—a joke? Some kind of novelty item?"

"No," I say, even though I don't know what he means by "novelty item." I'll have to ask Mom. Now I'm really starting to get ka-flooeyed, and I can hear my voice squeaking as I say, "They're chokers for *people.*"

Mr. Kumba heaves a deep sigh, then says, "Nobody is gonna wear these. Maybe a bunch of kids, but that's not my customer."

"Oh, okay," I say stuttering, then put the chokers back into the shopping bag as quick as I can, so we can do an abracadabra before I die of embarrassment.

"Thank you, for your time," Chuchie says sweetly, as we all make a mad dash for the door.

We're all real quiet on the way home. "I feel like I was just in a hot-air balloon flying over Oz, then someone let out the air," I mumble to Chuchie. We used to watch *The Wizard of Oz* together a kazillion times when we were kids.

"We're not in Oz, *para seguro,*" Chuchie

moans back, resting her head on my shoulder as we head uptown on the subway. Do' Re Mi, Aqua, and Angie get up to transfer to the West Side train.

"What do you call a mouse who eats at Mikki D's?" I yell to Aqua and Angie as they get off the train.

"I don't know, Galleria," Aqua says, looking kinda sad.

"Mikki Mouse," I say, smirking at my feeble joke. "Sleep tight, tonite."

"Thanks a lot, Galleria. We will!" Angie pipes up.

When they get off the train, I go right back to my sad face.

"What do grown-ups know, anyway?" Chuchie says, as I give her a hug good-bye.

"For true!" I agree, as she gets off at Prince Street to go home.

I ride uptown by myself. I reach into the shopping bag, and look at the Cheetah Girl chokers again. Fighting back the tears, I rub the smooth cheetah suede with my fingers.

I don't care what Mr. Bumbling Kumba says. These chokers are dope, even if I *am* at the end of my rope! After all, we can't all work that back-to-the-motherland look like he does in *his* store. But, God, please, get us a record deal before we end up homeless, selling broken-down chokers on the street!

Chapter 10

It's eight o'clock in the morning, and Dad has already left to go to work. Mom is almost ready to go to the store, because there is some drama. See, she designed all the bridal wear for L.A. rapper Tubby Rock's wedding party, but apparently the bride-to-be spent too much time at Aunt Kizzy's, eating barbecued baby back ribs!

"I can't believe Peta Rock went and gained ten pounds right before the wedding!" Mom says, sulking and spreading butter on her croissant.

I stand in the kitchen patiently, because I really need to talk to her, even though she's feeling ka-flooeyed. She was already sleeping when I got home last night. The truth is, I'm still gaspitating by what Mr. Kumba said about the Cheetah Girl chokers, and maybe he's right—who is gonna buy these things?

That's why I have to ask Mom—because I know if nothing else, she will tell me the truth. "What do you think?" I ask her with bated breath, showing off my choker.

"You look fierce," Mom says, looking up from the newspaper and glancing at me, then picking up her mochaccino latte and taking a sip.

I still don't move from the spot where I'm standing, and when Mom looks up again, I start motioning at my neck so she gets the drift.

"Darling, what am I supposed to be looking at?"

"Mom, the *choker*—I, we, made them yesterday," I insist, getting more nervous.

"What's it say? Oh, 'Growl Power'—ooh, that is too fierce," she says approvingly.

"Do you think people will wear them?" I ask her sheepishly.

"Well, I don't think grown-ups will wear them—God forbid they should get an original idea. They'd probably think it's a dog collar or something," Mom says, giggling.

She doesn't realize how crushed I am. Suddenly, I start sobbing, just like I used to do when I was little. I feel so silly willy, but I can't take any more rejection! Or maybe it's my hormones acting up.

Mom just sits there, until I tell her what happened at the Kumba boutique in Brooklyn last night. All of a sudden, she starts smiling, and asks, "Do you know why I opened the Toto in New York boutique?"

I'm not quite sure where she's going with this, but knowing Mom, she has a point to the joint. "Because you wanted to, right?" I respond.

"No—not at first. The only dream I had back then was to make diva-size clothes that would make skinny women pant with 'Gucci Envy.' So that's what I did. I designed a whole collection—and when I had about thirty designs or so, I made appointments with buyers at department stores."

Mom sips her mochaccino, her eyes sparkling. "Oh, I was so excited. I knew my clothes were fierce, and I thought the buyers would be *begging* me for orders. Do you know what happened?"

"No, Mom, what?" I ask, giggling now, because Mom sure knows how to drag out a story.

"Every single one of those buyers laughed me out of the store," Mom says, her eyes getting animated. "Not only didn't they buy *one* scraggly piece from my collection, but they told me that no 'large-size' woman would be caught *dead* in my clothes!"

"Really?" I ask, genuinely surprised. Mom never told me that happened to her!

"I was devastated beyond belief. I almost threw the clothes in the trash can after one appointment with a particularly shady buyer, I remember," she recalls, chuckling. "But I figured, I knew at least one large-size woman who *would* wear my clothes."

"Who was that?" I ask curiously.

"Me, of course," Mom says chuckling. "And if there was *one,* then there had to be *others*—they just didn't know it yet!"

"What do you mean?" I ask, puzzled.

"Well, sometimes people don't even know they want something until it's right before their eyes," Mom explains, nodding her head wisely.

Now I get her drift. It never occurred to me

that Mom's clothes were anything but fierce, and I can't believe that there were people who didn't think so back in the day!

"You gotta *make* people like your stuff, that's what you're saying?" I ask, feeling better already.

"*Exactement croissant,* darling," Mom says, speaking what she calls Poodle French. "Be prepared for a battle, though, at first. When I opened the doors of my boutique, it was so slow, I thought I was gonna lose my leopard bloomers! And believe me, there were plenty of people waiting for me to fail—talking behind my back, heckling outside the store. But eventually the divas found their way down the yellow brick road, and they've been clamoring at the door of Toto in New York ever since!"

"Thank you, Mom," I say, giving her a hug. And then I ask her what is really bothering me. "Are you gonna keep on being our manager, Mom?"

"Why, of course, Galleria—why wouldn't I?" Much to my relief, she looks surprised that I asked.

"Well, 'cuz it's causing so much drama . . .

and I know there's been trouble with the store . . ."

"Galleria," Mom stops me. "Darling, please— I always do what I want to do, don't I? Believe me, Toto in New York will survive and thrive. And someday, one day or another, I'm convinced that being the manager of the fabulous Cheetah Girls is gonna pay off—in full!"

"You really think so, Mom?"

"I know so," she says. "Def Duck may come through and quack, or it may not. But your dreams are gonna come true in the jiggy jungle, Galleria. Who knows— maybe you'll be the fashion queen of the Cheetah scene!"

I giggle with pleasure and relief. "Am I really that different from other girls, Mom?" I ask.

"I don't know, Galleria," Mom says seriously. "But I do know that you're special—if that's what you mean by different, then I guess so."

"I already got a few orders for the chokers in school," I tell her excitedly, forgetting my anxiety attack already.

"Really, darling?" Mom says smiling. "Do you need any help making them?"

"No, Mom, I *don't*!" I say, giggling, then pulling out the chokers we made last night. "We made these by ourselves. I didn't even let Dad stick his nimble fingers into our situation."

"All right, darling, don't get your bloomers in a bunch before lunch!"

Flinging my backpack on my shoulder, I kiss Mom on the forehead, then thank her for her advice. "We're gonna do what you said. We'll wear the chokers ourselves, till other peeps are panting like puppies for them!"

"Mm-hmm. I'm sure Toto will approve darling," Mom says, throwing me a kiss good-bye.

"Woof, there it is!" I giggle back, then run off to school.

On the way there, I'm thinking about my snap— that would make a dope song, I think— "Woof, There It Is!"

I whip out my Kitty Kat notebook, and start writing down a lyric. That's how I flow.

The Cheetah Girls may not have a record contract yet, and we may not have sold any chokers, either. But we're never gonna stop layin' down our global groove—not until the whole world comes pouncin' at our door! "Woof, There It Is!"

Woof, There It Is!

It takes five
To make the Cheetah Girls be,
Ah, yeah, can't you see
That they're rocking on a thing
Called the M.I.C.
The M.I.C., well that's a microphone
And when they rock it to the beat
It's rocked to the doggy bone.

Woof, there it is!
Woof, there it is!
Woof, there it is!

The Cheetah Girls Glossary

Always looking out: Representing. Watching your back.

As a matter of facto: It *really really* is true.

The bill: the lineup of performers for the evening or event.

Blacktress: Black movie star.

Boho: Black bohemian.

Bou bou fon fon: A bouffant hairstyle that's piled so high, it had to be done twice!

Cali: Los Angeles, California.

Cheetah-certified: When something is so "for true," you can take it to the bank, baby.

Cheetah-licious: Fierce, fiercer, fiercest!

The chillies: the creeps.

Coiffed: Hair that has been blow-dryed, blow-torched, and fussed-over at the beauty parlor!

Coinky-dinky: A coincidence.

Cracking face: Saying something stupid. Looking stupid.

Cruising altitude: When a plane has climbed

the distance it needs to fly the friendly skies until it reaches its destination.

Crustacean-looking slime: Something alien-like that pops out of noses or gets stuck in the corner of the mouth.

Déjà vu: A feeling that you've been somewhere before.

Exactement croissant: Poodle French for "That's right."

Fabbie-poo: beyond fabulous

Flexing fowl: Put your foot in your mouth.

Fowl like a nearsighted owl: Wack.

Flipping the script: Turning the tables, changing the subject.

Freaked it: Rocked the mic.

Fugly: Beyond ugly.

Goospitating: Shrieking inside. Getting squeamish about something.

Hooptie: a car

Kadoodling: Wasting precious time. Angling for something.

Kaflempt, Ka-flooeyed: *Really really* exasperated.

La La Land: Los Angeles, California

Let's do an abracadabra: Let's scram! Do a disappearing act.

Madrina: Godmother, but not to be confused with fairy godmother who pays for everything!

Manny-hanny: Manhattan

Milks it for points: When you act cheesy just to get attention.

Minnie-Mouse Minute: When time stands still for so long, you're ka-flooeyed to the max!

Okeydokey: A flim-flam situation.

On the dis tip: Kinda playing the dozens, or "snapping" to and fro.

On the d.l.: On the "down low," or sneak tip.

Op: Opportunity, which sometimes only knocks once!

Out-kadoodled: Out-foxed by a cheetah.

Paying the Boogie Man in full: When you're more scared than when a vampire jumps out of a coffin and runs after you with his bloody arm!

Rocked to the doggy bone: Performing to the max.

Scemo: Bozo. Pronounced like "shame-o."

Schemer: Finagler. Player.

Snaggled-tooth haggling: Bargaining someone down till you draw blood!

Stinkeroon: When something stinks.

Stop faking that you're not quaking: Stop pretending that you're not scared.

Supa-packed itinerary: Busy schedule.

Taking off points: Reading someone.

Thank gooseness: Thank goodness.

That's so radikkio: Don't try it, Miss Thingy. You know that's ridiculous!

That's the deal-io, yo: That's the way it is.

The Twilight Zone: A weird place where weird things are happening and time seems to stand still.

Venue: A location where acts will appear to perform.

A visit to freak city: Flipping out from fear.

Woof, there it is!: When you know you've rocked it to the doggy bone and you can step back and say, "How you like me now?"

Work your spots till they're dots!: Be your fiercest self until it's time to close the lid on the coffin.

PHOTO BY CHARLIE PIZZARELLO

ABOUT THE AUTHOR

Deborah Gregory earned her growl power as a diva-about-town contributing writer for ESSENCE, VIBE, and MORE magazines. She has showed her spots on several talk shows, including OPRAH, RICKI LAKE, and MAURY POVICH. She lives in New York City with her pooch, Cappuccino, who is featured as the Cheetah Girls' mascot, Toto.

PHOTO BY TREVOR BROWN

JUMP AT THE SUN